ARNOLD
SCHWARZENEGGER

ARNOLD
SCHWARZENEGGER

LARGER THAN LIFE

Craig A. Doherty and Katherine M. Doherty

Walker and Company
New York

First published in the United States of America in 1993 by Walker Publishing Company, Inc.

Published simultaneously in Canada by Thomas Allen & Son Canada, Limited, Markham, Ontario

Library of Congress Cataloging-in-Publication Data
Doherty, Craig A.
Arnold Schwarzenegger : larger than life / Craig A. Doherty and Katherine M. Doherty.
p. cm.
Includes bibliographical references (p.   ) and index.
Summary: Describes the childhood, bodybuilding career, and motion picture achievements of the popular celebrity.
ISBN 0-8027-8236-1.—ISBN 0-8027-8238-8 (lib. ed.)
1. Schwarzenegger, Arnold—Juvenile literature.   2. Bodybuilders—United States—Biography—Juvenile literature.   3. Actors—United States—Biography—Juvenile literature.   [1. Schwarzenegger, Arnold.   2. Bodybuilders.   3. Actors and actresses.]   I. Doherty, Katherine M.   II. Title.
GV545.52.S38D64   1993
646.7'5'092—dc20
[B]   93-17469
CIP
AC

The list of Arnold Schwarzenegger's bodybuilding titles in Appendix One, page 105, appears courtesy of George Butler, from his book, Arnold Schwarzenegger: A Portrait.

Printed in the United States of America

2   4   6   8   10   9   7   5   3   1

Contents

ARNOLD
SCHWARZENEGGER

Introduction

"That which does not kill us makes us stronger." In the fantasy world of motion pictures these words of the philosopher Nietzsche, from the opening of *Conan the Barbarian,* have defined the many roles that Arnold Schwarzenegger has played. Starting with *Conan,* Arnold Schwarzenegger has had an unprecedented run of thirteen box office hits. His movies grossed over a billion dollars in the 1980s. Schwarzenegger was paid around $25 million for his most recent movie, *The Last Action Hero.*

Along the way he has been attacked by wolves, required stitches, and was almost set on fire by an overzealous stunt coordinator. The characters he has portrayed have overcome every type of bad guy imaginable. From the snake-cult leader

Arnold Schwarzenegger

Thulsa Doom to the seemingly indestructible T-1000, the good guys have won. Arnold's movies have demanded that the motion picture industry provide viewers with better and more spectacular special effects. It is no longer enough to mount a camera on the front of a car and go careening through traffic. Computer-generated effects that astound the mind and the eye have become the expectation of the audience, not the exception.

It is the American dream come true when a police officer's son from a little town in Austria can start lifting weights to improve his body and end up being a friend and appointee of an American president. It is not by chance, though, that this happened. Arnold had a burning desire to be the best. From this desire he developed a plan—a plan that made him the greatest bodybuilder of his time and the most well-known celebrity in the world.

Chapter One

■

Arnold Schwarzenegger, the Boy

▓ ▓ ▓ ▓ ▓ ▓

O~n~ July 30, 1947, Arnold Schwarzenegger was born to Gustav and Aurelia Schwarzenegger. His father was the chief of police in the small Austrian town of Thal, a farming and lumbering community of approximately 1,200 people near Graz, Austria's second-largest city. The Schwarzeneggers lived in the second story of a 300-year-old stone house. The house was an official residence and came with the position of chief of police.

This part of Austria is very conservative and traditional. When Arnold was growing up, many people still wore their traditional outfits on a regular basis, and they are still worn today on special occasions. Aurelia Schwarzenegger did the cooking, cleaning, and shopping for the household, which often meant that she would walk from farm to farm buying what was needed.

In many ways, Arnold's early years were no different from those of other people growing up in Europe after World War II. Times were hard. Meat was a rarity in the Schwarzenegger diet, on the menu about once a week. The Schwarzeneggers did without indoor plumbing, a refrigerator, or a telephone until Arnold was in his teens. One distinctive aspect of Arnold's early years was the role his father played in the family.

Gustav Schwarzenegger had been a military man before becoming a policeman and had found the discipline and regimentation of the military appealing. It has been reported in many places that Gustav ran his family with military-style discipline. And although Arnold rebelled against his father's ideas, the discipline Arnold learned from his father served him well when it came to the rigors of training for bodybuilding competitions.

Arnold learned early that he didn't like losing. Gustav continually pitted Arnold against his brother, Meinhard, who was a year older. They competed in boxing matches, ski races, soccer, and any other sporting events their father could think of. Gustav would humiliate the loser, usually Arnold, by forcing him to answer the question of who was the better competitor.

Gustav's strict discipline was not restricted to athletics. Both boys were required to do chores to "earn" their breakfast each morning before school. The Schwarzeneggers were practicing Catholics and the boys were required to attend mass every Sunday. After church, the family would go to concerts where Gustav played in a local band, visit museums, and attend other cultural events. After these family outings, Arnold and Meinhard each had to write a ten-page report on the day's trip. Gustav would then read and correct the reports. Any misspelled words had to be correctly written fifty times, so Arnold and Meinhard wrote these papers very carefully.

Another influence on young Arnold was the movies. His favorite movies were the series of Hercules movies that starred bodybuilders American Steve Reeves, South African Reg Park, and others. Arnold took those adolescent dreams of being the strongest, the biggest, and the hero, and turned them into reality.

As a child, Arnold tried many sports, hoping to find one at which he could excel. In the December 1977 issue of *Family Health* Arnold said that "from the time I was 10 years old, I wanted to be the very best at something. . . . I had visions of being really great."[1] Like most European children, Arnold played soccer. By the age of twelve, he was a wing for the Graz Athletic Club, reportedly the second-best team in the city.

When Arnold was fifteen he was set on the path that would lead him to a level of success that even he couldn't have imagined. His soccer coach started taking the team into a gym on a regular basis so they could use weights to strengthen their leg muscles for soccer. Arnold had always wanted to be the best at something and training with weights seemed to be it. Arnold was already six feet tall, but weighed only 150 pounds. It was not long before his tall, lanky body began to fill out.

In his book *Arnold: The Education of a Bodybuilder* he wrote about his first real workout at the gym.[2] He had ridden his bike the eight miles from his house in Thal to the gym in Graz. After the workout his muscles were so sore he fell off his bike and ended up pushing it home. By the next morning he couldn't get his muscles to do simple tasks like comb his hair and hold a coffee cup. Despite his mother's concerns, Arnold was soon back in the gym. Although he did excel at other sports, it wasn't long before he had dropped out of most of his other activities to concentrate on bodybuilding. In 1964 he became the city and national junior curling champion while at the same time Gustav became the senior champion. Curling is a sport that combines aspects of bowling and shuffleboard. It is played on ice within a 14-foot-by-138-foot area. A forty-eight-pound circular stone with a handle is slid the length of the lane. The one who comes closest to a one-foot circle at the other end wins the point.

Arnold, however, wanted more than the limited exposure the sport of curling would give him. He still had the image firmly planted in his mind of himself as the next Reg Park. Soon he was spending every free moment in the gym lifting weights. He would either walk or ride his bike the eight miles to and from the gym. His parents became concerned about his apparent obsession and limited him to going to the gym only three times a week. To make up for his lost time in the gym, Arnold fixed up a room in an unheated part of their house as a weight room. He would work out in there when he couldn't go to the gym in Graz. Arnold would train in his unheated home gym even when the temperature outside was below zero. In 1965, after graduating from secondary school, Arnold Schwarzenegger began the next chapter in his life.

Chapter Two

■

Bodybuilder-Soldier

▓ ▓ ▓ ▓ ▓ ▓

As Arnold became a regular at the gym he also became part of the cadre of dedicated body-builders in the Graz area. He was the youngest of this group and received a lot of help and encouragement from his older friends. Arnold especially credits Dr. Karl Gerstl with helping him get started on the program that helped him develop his body's potential. Arnold had the perfectly proportioned skeletal frame on which he could eventually sculpt the perfect body.

In October 1965, Arnold went into the Austrian army for a year to fulfill his mandatory military service. Arnold has claimed that this was the first time he was fed meat at every meal. That diet helped him go from 200 to 225 pounds. While in his first month of basic training, Arnold received an invita-

Arnold Schwarzenegger

tion to his first bodybuilding competition. The Mr. Europe, Junior was to be held in Stuttgart, Germany, on October 30, 1965. The army only let people leave during basic training if there was a death in the family or some other major emergency. There would be no leave granted for a bodybuilding competition.

When it came time for the competition Arnold was determined to be there. He jumped the fence and went AWOL, absent without leave. He had barely enough money to buy a very inexpensive third-class ticket to Stuttgart. When he got there he had to borrow posing trunks and body oil from one of the other competitors. He really had no idea of how to pose except for what he had seen in the various muscle magazines that he read whenever he could and what he could remember of the pictures of Reg Park with which he had covered his room. Pictures of him at this time show a tall, well-proportioned young man with excellent symmetry. Yet his body lacked the mass and definition that would make him famous. To the educated eyes of some in the bodybuilding world, it was a body with great potential.

The trip turned out to be worth the risk as Arnold Schwarzenegger was named Mr. Europe, Junior for 1965. He was caught as he climbed back over the fence to get back on base and was put in a military jail for seven days. His superiors were impressed, however, when they heard he had won the Mr. Europe, Junior title. When he got out of jail and for the rest of the time he was in the army, he was given time to work out in a gym. His victory in Stuttgart gave him the incentive and confidence to go on. And from that point Arnold never looked back. His mind was focused on one thing: becoming the greatest bodybuilder that ever lived.

Bodybuilding is an often misunderstood activity. Some people regard it as nothing more than a version of a beauty pageant while others see it as a sport. In terms of the physical exertion it takes to reach the highest levels, it is possibly the most demanding of all sports. At the same time, the best bodybuilders are also the best performers. The objective of bodybuilding is to sculpt your muscles into the most perfect size and shape for your skeletal frame. Each and every muscle in the body ideally can be seen as a separate entity in perfect proportion to the muscles around it. With the exception until recently of the United States, bodybuilding competitions are major sporting events attracting large crowds all over the world. Arnold Schwarzenegger is almost singlehandedly responsible for the growth of interest in bodybuilding in the United States.

The origins of bodybuilding can be traced back in time to the ancient Greeks. In more modern times it can be traced to the Prussians in the early nineteenth century. After they were defeated by Napoleon, Prussia was disarmed. The men of the country began forming clubs to strengthen their bodies, as their bodies were the only weapons they had.

With his father's influence, Arnold was assigned to tank training, an honor that was usually restricted to young men over the age of twenty-one, while Arnold was only eighteen. Arnold enjoyed driving tanks but was much more interested in bodybuilding. When he was excused from afternoon duties, he began spending six hours a day in the army gym.

Before going into the army, Arnold had competed as a successful Olympic powerlifter and had won the Austrian junior weight-lifting championship. But he didn't pursue this. Powerlifters do not concern themselves with developing perfect bodies. Their only concern is to be as strong as they can for the limited movements needed to do the "snatch" and the "clean and jerk" with hundreds of pounds on the bar. Once he won the Mr. Europe, Junior title, Arnold concentrated on bodybuilding.

One person at the Mr. Europe, Junior contest was so impressed with Arnold Schwarzenegger that he offered Arnold a job in his Munich health and bodybuilding gym when Arnold got out of the army. This person also offered to send Arnold to the next Mr. Universe contest in London so he could see what the top bodybuilders were doing. Arnold wanted to go to London, but not as an observer. He expected to be ready to compete with the best in the world by the time the Mr. Universe contest rolled around in September 1966. One other person that Arnold met in Stuttgart was an Italian powerlifter from the island of Sardinia, off the coast of Italy. This person, Franco Columbo, was five feet five inches tall and six years older than Arnold. By the time he met Arnold in Stuttgart he had ridden in horse races in Italy and been the lightweight boxing champion of Italy. He was in Stuttgart competing in a powerlifting contest.

In August 1966, Arnold was finished with his army training and became the manager of Putziger's Gym in Munich. Franco was also living in Munich. At first Arnold had a hard time adjusting to his role of club manager. He found it hard to meet the demands of the members and still devote adequate time to his own training. It was at this time that he started to split his workouts, working two hours in the morning and two hours in the evening. Arnold claimed that by splitting his workouts he didn't get as tired and was able to lift more weight. He would work on his arms and shoulders in the morning and then for a few hours work with the customers in the gym. During the day he would eat two heavy meals. When he would go back to the gym in the evening, he would train his abdominals, chest, and legs. The split workout has become standard procedure for serious bodybuilders all over the world.

During his first year in Munich he spent much of his free time going out with women, drinking, and fighting in the beer halls of Munich. Reportedly Arnold was better known at this time for his skills as a barroom brawler than as a bodybuilder.

Despite his wild times that first year in Munich, Arnold won the Mr. Europe title and the Best Built Man in Europe contest. He and Franco also competed in the International Powerlifting Championship. Arnold wanted to prove that one could be a bodybuilder and still be strong. There was no question—Franco won the middleweight title and Arnold won the heavyweight division. He lifted 485 pounds in the bench press, 550 in the squat, 710 in the dead lift, for a total of 1,745 pounds.

Even with his growing success in bodybuilding, Arnold did not receive the support of his family at this time. His mother would write to him asking him to come home and do something practical, like become a carpenter. Little did she or anyone else realize at that time that Arnold was on the verge of becoming the most successful bodybuilder in the history of the sport. He would soon surpass the accomplishments of all the bodybuilders he admired, including Reg Park, his idol.

The next hurdle on Arnold Schwarzenegger's horizon was the Mr. Universe contest held in London. Although there had been promises of sponsorship for the trip to London, they did not materialize. The sponsors of the Mr. Europe contest had offered to send Arnold to London but withdrew the offer when Arnold entered and won the Best Built Man in Europe contest, which was sanctioned by a rival bodybuilding organization. Like many sports, bodybuilding is split among a number of sponsoring organizations that often disagree more than they get along.

Arnold Schwarzenegger

Arnold was finally able to raise enough money to go to London and compete in the NABBA (National Amateur British Bodybuilding Association) Mr. Universe contest in 1966. He was still, at nineteen, very much the Austrian country boy, and remembers thinking as he fastened his seat belt, " 'What if it crashes and I never get there?' And when I heard the landing gear come up with a shudder into the body of the plane, it was like a cold fist closing on my heart. I was certain we were gone."[1]

Chapter Three
Mr. Universe and Beyond

When Arnold arrived in London, in September 1966, he hardly spoke any English. He had memorized one line: "I would like to go to the Royal Hotel, please." It worked like a charm except for one thing. There are two Royal Hotels in London and he ended up at the wrong one. Fortunately he soon found the right one.

Arnold had made great progress in the past year in Munich. There wasn't another European bodybuilder who could beat him. Arnold arrived in London confident that he could win—until he saw Chet Yorton from the United States. The Europeans were definitely behind the Americans in the level of overall completeness of their bodies. Arnold first saw Chet Yorton as

Yorton came out of an elevator Arnold was waiting to get into. One look at Yorton and Arnold felt defeated.

In bodybuilding the major portion of the judging takes place prior to the public performance. Usually the judging is done in the afternoon and then the competition is open to the public the next evening. During the afternoon each contestant is judged individually through a series of standard poses that allow the judges to examine each and every muscle group in the body. The evening pose-off, which is what most people are familiar with, plays a much smaller role in the decision of the judges. Arnold was one of the audience's favorites at the 1966 Mr. Universe, but the judges gave the title to Yorton. Although disappointed, Arnold used this contest as a learning experience. He realized that as good as he was in comparison to the other European bodybuilders, he had a lot of hard work ahead of him if he wanted to be able to beat the best of the Americans. He also realized the power of the psych-out. Even if he could have beaten Yorton physically, he had allowed Yorton to beat him mentally. Arnold was quick to realize that in a close contest the mental aspects of competing were extremely important. Arnold became a master of the mental competition. He made sure he was mentally ready to win, and did what he could to upset the mental strategies of his opponents.

But Arnold still had weaknesses at this point in his career: His posing lacked polish. It was still a mix borrowed from other competitors and from pictures in the muscle magazines and was not planned to fully complement his attributes. Arnold felt he could have beaten Yorton had he not only been stronger mentally but been better prepared to pose as well. This realization gave him the added incentive to work even harder than he had before.

Wag Bennett, an English bodybuilding enthusiast, had been

especially impressed with Arnold Schwarzenegger. Bennett had been one of the judges at the Mr. Universe contest who had reportedly put Arnold ahead of Yorton. Bennett invited Arnold to London later in the fall of 1966 to do some bodybuilding exhibitions. Bennett got Arnold to pose to music, something Arnold thought was rather foolish at first. But as Arnold overcame his inhibitions, he realized how much more impact his posing had on an audience when it flowed logically with the music, hitting his best poses as the music peaked. Bennett had used the music from the movie *Exodus*. Soon Arnold had his own copy and carried it around to use for all his exhibitions.

Arnold traveled around England on an exhibition tour that was so successful he was asked to do the same in Holland and Belgium. Arnold received very little money for his exhibitions, but he wasn't worried about that. The exposure was helping him and giving him confidence. Arnold had bought the gym he had managed in Munich and the membership now swelled to 200 in the wake of his growing reputation.

Coming in second in the Mr. Universe contest had given Arnold the confidence to begin corresponding with his idol, Reg Park. He soon learned that Park would be in London in January 1967 to do some exhibitions. Wag Bennett arranged for Arnold to be part of Park's tour. Arnold truly was in awe of Park. He wrote down much of the advice that Park offered so he could remember it and use it when he got back to Munich. Park turned out to be a positive role model for Arnold. After meeting Park, Arnold knew that all that really mattered to him was winning bodybuilding competitions. He wanted to be the best bodybuilder in the world, and he realized that drinking and fighting were counterproductive to his goals. He then abandoned his bad-boy role in the beer halls of Munich. The nineteen-year-old Arnold Schwarzenegger settled down to the work of making himself the best.

To become the very best, Arnold used a number of strategies, both mental and physical. He knew he had the right bone structure on which to build the best possible body and began to analyze his weak points. European bodybuilders of the time emphasized their upper bodies and neglected their legs. Arnold realized that his legs were one of the few negatives in his overall development and worked hard to improve them. He also worked hard on the mental aspects of bodybuilding. He removed as many distractions as possible from his training and began to practice the mental skills of visualization and affirmation.

To use visualization Arnold would picture himself in competition, keeping the expression on his face blank as he went through his posing routine, destroying the competition. He would visualize himself winning. He would also keep a list of affirmations written down that included such statements as: "You can handle yourself. You are confident. You are good." He would repeat these and other statements over and over before he would go to sleep each night and at other times during the day. He would tell himself that he was good, that he was a winner. By this time Arnold knew he was destined for great things. What distinguished him from others who imagined themselves doing great things was that Arnold was willing to make the sacrifices and put in the hard work that was necessary to accomplish his goals. He had one other incentive as he trained for the 1967 Mr. Universe contest: Reg Park had offered Arnold an invitation to come to South Africa and do an exhibition with him if Arnold won the Mr. Universe title.

During his training for the 1967 Mr. Universe competition in London, Arnold became concerned with working his body so that there would be separation between each and every muscle. He worked to eliminate every ounce of fat that filled the spaces between the muscles.

As Arnold continued to prepare for the next Mr. Universe contest, he became aware of another rising young star in bodybuilding: Dennis Tinnerino. From the pictures in the magazines Arnold knew that Tinnerino would be the one to beat in London in 1967. Arnold could see that Tinnerino had better legs than he did, which inspired Arnold to work even harder on his own legs. His ability to look at his own body with an objective eye was one of Arnold's greatest training aids. He could look in the mirror and see where he needed work. Arnold always had a realistic image of himself and his competition.

As Arnold arrived in London for the 1967 Mr. Universe competition, he was the favorite. As a bodybuilder, he had developed in the year since he had come in second to Yorton. He was bigger and better than he had been the year before, and he was a polished performer now. He was mentally ready to win. And he did.

At twenty years old, Arnold Schwarzenegger became the youngest man ever to win a Mr. Universe title. His victory was dampened by only two things. The first was the realization that the NABBA (National Amateur British Bodybuilding Association) Mr. Universe, Amateur title was only one of three Mr. Universe titles. Arnold was the NABBA amateur champion. There was also a professional NABBA Mr. Universe and there was a third Mr. Universe contest sponsored by the IFBB (International Federation of Bodybuilders), which was controlled by Joe and Ben Weider. The second negative was the reaction from his family back in Thal, which was less enthusiastic than Arnold had hoped for. Positive reaction did come from Reg

Park, who, good as his word, invited Arnold to South Africa for a visit and to do an exhibition.

In South Africa, Arnold was impressed with the elegance of the Parks' home. Although Park praised Arnold for his accomplishments, he also critiqued Arnold's body and training techniques. Arnold was especially impressed with the amount of weight Park used in training his calves, Arnold's weakest point. Inspired now by Park and his own success, Arnold returned to Munich to train even harder. Things were going well and membership in Arnold's club was now up to 400.

Arnold's next goal was to win the 1968 NABBA professional Mr. Universe title. He upped his workouts to two and a half hours twice a day. Once a week he and a training partner would "shock train" a specific group of muscles. They would take their weights out into the woods outside of Munich, pick one exercise, and do it for hours at a time.

In September 1968, Arnold became the winner of his second Mr. Universe title: This time he was the NABBA professional champion. After his victory, Joe Weider invited him to come to the United States and compete in the IFBB Mr. Universe competition that was to be held later in September 1968. Arnold knew that opportunity for him in Europe was limited. He later told George Butler that the rich and important people in Europe "make it very difficult for me and my friends to get ahead. . . . They despise us and stop us every step of the way." Arnold also told Butler that he felt differently about the United States. ". . . I go to America. You have opportunities."[1]

Chapter Four

∎

Off to America

If Arnold Schwarzenegger can be considered the king of bodybuilding, then Joe Weider is the kingmaker. Weider is the publisher of a variety of bodybuilding magazines. His brother, Ben, is the president of the International Federation of Bodybuilders (IFBB). The IFBB is an organization that sponsors many bodybuilding competitions including Mr. Olympia and the IFBB version of Mr. Universe. In addition to his publishing empire, Joe Weider also markets a vast array of bodybuilding equipment and dietary supplements.

But Joe Weider's greatest contribution to the sport of bodybuilding has probably been in picking out the talented young bodybuilders. He would give them the opportunity to train full-time in exchange for endorsement contracts. Arnold Schwarzenegger was to become one of his protégés.

When Weider invited Arnold to the Mr. Universe contest in Miami, Florida, he also suggested that Arnold plan to stay in the United States and train in California. Part of Arnold's dream had been to become a movie star like Reeves and Park. Weider's offer was definitely a step in the right direction if Arnold Schwarzenegger's plan was to be realized. Arnold would tell anyone who would listen of his plan to become the world's greatest bodybuilder, move to America, own property, star in movies, and marry a rich and beautiful woman. At the time, many scoffed at Arnold's dream, but in retrospect it is amazing how close to reality it was.

Arnold went to Miami full of confidence, expecting to win his third Mr. Universe title. There were many bodybuilders at the contest whom Arnold knew and many more that he had only seen in the muscle magazines. Arnold's confidence remained strong throughout the contest. It wasn't until the pose-off that he realized how close the contest was. Something happened that stunned Arnold. He was called for second place and Frank Zane, who had been first in the medium class, was given the title.

Although Arnold took the defeat hard he was forced into the realization that although he was the biggest, he was not yet the best. Zane had beat him because his muscles were better defined and his overall symmetry was better. Arnold quickly recovered from the defeat and renewed his efforts to become the undisputed best in the bodybuilding world. And now he would also be training with the best. Weider offered him a small apartment in Santa Monica, California, along with a car and one hundred dollars a week. Arnold would be free to train full time. In exchange for this, Weider received the rights to use pictures of Arnold in his magazines. In addition, Arnold would reveal his training regimen in articles to be published in Weider's magazines.

Life in California agreed with Arnold. He found it to be the perfect place to train. Arnold first trained with Vince Gironda, whose gym was on Ventura Boulevard near Universal City. Arnold then switched to Gold's Gym in Santa Monica, where many of the best bodybuilders in the world trained. During his training in 1969, Arnold concentrated on improving the "cuts," or muscle definition, of his muscles. The 1969 IFBB Mr. Universe contest was held in New York in the fall. Arnold became the undisputed winner of the Mr. Universe title, receiving first place from all seven judges.

There was still one major bodybuilder Arnold hadn't beaten and that was Sergio Oliva, known in bodybuilding circles as the Myth. Oliva was not at the Mr. Universe contest: He was across town competing in the Mr. Olympia contest. At the last minute, Arnold Schwarzenegger decided to compete head to head, muscle to muscle against the Myth. Oliva was so dominant that no one had shown up to compete against him at the 1968 Mr. Olympia contest. He would not get off so easily in 1969.

The 1969 Mr. Olympia contest has been reported as one of the greatest confrontations in the history of bodybuilding. Oliva was the established star, apparently the undisputed king. Arnold Schwarzenegger was an upstart, a would-be usurper of Oliva's crown. The crowd that night had come to see Oliva and were stunned to utter silence when Arnold Schwarzenegger struck his first pose. The crowd remained silent through the first few poses and then went wild. When Arnold left the stage, the crowd chanted for more but Arnold did not return. After the applause for Arnold stopped, a chant for Oliva began and lasted for five minutes until he arrived on stage. When Oliva finally took the stage and struck his first pose the audience reacted with pandemonium. When Oliva left the stage the judges had seen the two greatest bodies ever presented on one stage. The king and the crown prince of bodybuilding. Whether they truly couldn't make up their minds or they were just playing to the audience's enthusiasm is unknown. The judges called for Arnold and Oliva to return to the stage together for one last look.

Sergio Oliva won the Mr. Olympia contest that night with the seven judges splitting four to three in his favor. Arnold never argued that decision: He felt Oliva deserved the win. In fact, Arnold felt he had lost the competition in the dressing room before it began. In Rick Wayne's book, *Muscle Wars*, Arnold says of Oliva,

> After he'd pumped up and undressed, I couldn't believe what I saw. Then Sergio walked past me and spread out his lats, ever so casually, you understand, but that was enough to freeze my blood. Right there and then I knew it was all over for me. I was completely psyched out.[1]

In addition to the title, Sergio Oliva also won the distinction of being the last person ever to beat Arnold Schwarzenegger in a bodybuilding contest. The next week Arnold was in London to successfully defend his NABBA Mr. Universe title. At twenty-two, it was his second Mr. Universe title in a year and his fourth overall. The crown prince would now ascend to the throne.

As if his rigorous training and competition weren't enough, 1969 was an important year for Arnold in other ways. Franco Columbo moved to California and the two friends were reunited. Franco at first shared Arnold's tiny apartment until they found a larger two-bedroom apartment in Santa Monica. In the

Off to America

summer of 1969, Arnold also began his first serious relationship with a woman. He started dating Barbara Outland, who was waitressing for the summer at a restaurant in Santa Monica called Zucky's. Barbara was to be a senior at San Diego State in the fall. After she returned to school, she would come and spend weekends with Arnold in Santa Monica.

In the fall of 1969, after the major competitions, a movie was being made in New York for Italian TV. They were looking for someone to play the title role. The producers contacted Joe Weider looking for someone to be Hercules in *Hercules Goes Bananas*. Weider reportedly misled them, saying he had an actor who had done Shakespeare in Germany. Weider showed up at the interview with Arnold Schwarzenegger in tow. Arnold had been instructed to let Weider do the talking. Arnold got the job and at Weider's suggestion used the stage name of Arnold Strong. Weider felt that the name Schwarzenegger was too much for Americans to deal with. Arnold received $1,000 a week for the twelve weeks of shooting. It didn't matter that Arnold couldn't speak English well because the film was to be dubbed in Italian.

The title of the film was changed to *Hercules in New York* and in 1970 it was redubbed in English and released in the United States. The movie has the rather preposterous story line of an angry Greek god, Zeus, sending Hercules to modern New York City as punishment. In New York, Hercules is confronted with gangsters, bears, professional wrestlers, and even has a chariot race through Times Square. The movie languished in obscurity until it was re-released years later to try to cash in on Arnold's popularity as a movie star. The $12,000 that Arnold received for the movie was invested in real estate in southern California. Arnold would eventually own millions of dollars'

Arnold Schwarzenegger

worth of real estate including a commercial property in Denver, Colorado, that recently sold for $10 million.

From the end of 1969 and for the next few years, one wonders if there was more than one Arnold Schwarzenegger. In addition to training twice a day he was managing his real estate holdings, starting a mail order business, running a bricklaying business with Franco, and taking business classes.

Arnold's mail order business was part of the self-promotion that Arnold has become well known for. In the beginning he was selling Arnold T-shirts and photos as well as booklets with titles like "How Arnold Builds His Chest Like a Fortress." Barbara Outland helped Arnold with the massive amounts of paperwork that were involved in running the business.

The bricklaying business was advertised as "European bricklayers, expert work." Reportedly Franco was the expert and Arnold handled the business end of things. As a result of an earthquake they were overwhelmed with work, mainly rebuilding chimneys. At one point they reportedly had sixteen people working for them. Later, when Arnold was involved with the book and movie *Pumping Iron*, it was claimed that the bricklaying company had been called "Pumping Bricks." Although it sounded good, some say it was just part of the hype for the book and movie.[2]

In 1970 Arnold started taking business courses. He was near the top of the bodybuilding world, if not already there, and had starred in *Hercules in New York*. Arnold was looking ahead, however, and realized that if he wanted long-term financial security he would have to have a better understanding of the business world. For some time, because Arnold didn't have a student visa, he could only take two classes at any one school. He took classes at Santa Monica City College, West Los Angeles College, UCLA, and others. Barbara would help with his research. Although Arnold had trouble keeping up with the reading he is reported as being a bright student. Eventually he discovered, through his association with the Special Olympics, a program at the University of Wisconsin in Superior that would allow him credit for all his various courses. He still needed ten more credits, which he took, and received a bachelor's degree in business and international economics in 1979 from the University of Wisconsin.

Through all this Arnold was improving himself as a bodybuilder. He had switched gyms and was working out at Gold's, running and tanning on the beach in Santa Monica. He even took ballet lessons to improve his posing routines. It all paid off. "He was in rock hard condition, every body part sharply defined, as if a master sculptor had produced his overall symmetry."[3] In the fall of 1970 Arnold was ready to take on all comers, and like the movie characters he would come to play, he vanquished all his opponents.

Chapter Five

Mr. Everything

In the short span of time between September 18 and October 3, 1970, Arnold Schwarzenegger won three major bodybuilding competitions. He also eliminated all doubt from anyone's mind that he was the ultimate bodybuilder.

A bittersweet moment occurred on September 18, 1970. Arnold was once again in London to defend his NABBA professional Mr. Universe title. His major competition would be Reg Park. It had been twenty years since the South African Park had first burst onto the bodybuilding scene. He had spent the last year in the gym planning to make a comeback. But Arnold was there, and Park's comeback fizzled. Although Park came in second, pictures of the two show that Park's conditioning wasn't even close to Arnold's.

As soon as the curtain came down, Arnold was on a plane to New York. The Pro Mr. World contest was to take place the next day in Columbus, Ohio. Arnold, much to the surprise of many, would be there. Sergio Oliva had been talked into competing in the contest in part because he assumed that Arnold would not be able to be there. He knew he would meet Arnold in New York at the Mr. Universe contest in two weeks but was not prepared to do so in Columbus. It seemed impossible for Arnold to compete one day in London, England, and the next in Ohio. But the organizers of the event chartered a plane to pick up Arnold in New York and get him to the competition on time.

The Mr. World contest came down to Dave Draper, Franco Columbo, Sergio Oliva, and the surprise contestant, Arnold Schwarzenegger. The judges, the audience, and the other competitors saw the difference: Oliva was not sharp. He had put on too much oil, and his muscles looked blurred in the mirrorlike reflection of light. Oliva's posing routine was also too short. Arnold, on the other hand, was perfect. The Myth's reign had come to an end.

There would be two weeks in the gym before the Mr. Olympia contest. In one interview Arnold had cautioned a reporter that he had to guard against becoming overconfident because a lot can happen in two weeks in the gym. But Arnold had not only become the master of his body, sculpting it with tons of iron; he had also become the master of the mental game. No one would ever psych out Arnold Schwarzenegger again, as Oliva had done in 1969. From now on Arnold would do the psyching out. Arnold's surprise arrival at Columbus may very well have been a carefully planned psychological assault on the Myth.

After the contest, the mental games began for the Mr. Olympia competition. Arnold reportedly told Oliva during a postcontest dinner that had Oliva weighed another ten pounds he would have beaten Arnold. If this was a ploy, it seemed to work. Oliva showed up at the Mr. Olympia competition with his finely chiseled muscles lost in an extra fifteen pounds of fat.

Even with the extra weight, however, Sergio Oliva gave Arnold a fight. Oliva, a transplanted Cuban who lived and trained in Chicago, had a huge following in New York. Despite his loss in Columbus, Oliva was still favored by many to win the Mr. Olympia title. As the defending champion, Oliva was accorded the honor of posing last.

After Oliva had posed, he, Reg Lewis, and Arnold Schwarzenegger were called back on stage. The judges looked them over and quickly eliminated Lewis, leaving Arnold and Oliva head to head, muscle to muscle. According to Rick Wayne in his book *Muscle Wars*, after posing together for a while Arnold turned to Oliva. He told him he was getting tired and suggested they leave the stage. Oliva agreed, dropped his hands, and left. The audience booed his departure and Arnold stayed on stage striking another pose, turning Oliva's boos into cheers for himself. We will never know if that was another master stroke in the psychological warfare practiced at the top levels of bodybuilding. Arnold was declared the winner of the 1970 professional Mr. Olympia competition. His claim to the throne of bodybuilding was now complete.

Although Arnold was now at the top of his bodybuilding career, things were not going well for the rest of his family. In May 1971 Arnold's older brother, Meinhard, was killed in a car crash. Meinhard had been drinking heavily and was killed instantly when he drove into another car. Years later Arnold was quoted as saying he had expected something to happen to Meinhard because he had always lived on the edge. Meinhard left behind his three-year-old son, Patrick. At first Patrick lived with his maternal grandparents because his mother, Erika Knapp, could not afford to raise him. Later on, Patrick would live with his mother and her new husband in Lisbon. Arnold Schwarzenegger helped support Patrick financially, and paid for Patrick to go to a private high school in Lisbon. Later Arnold brought Patrick to the United States, where he went to college and lives in a house that belongs to Arnold.

Nineteen seventy-one brought some rumblings in the bodybuilding world. The IFBB, in an attempt to gain total control of the sport, banned any competitors from IFBB competitions who had participated in a competition not sanctioned by the IFBB. This forced Arnold into choosing whether to defend his Mr. Universe title or his Mr. Olympia title. He chose the more prestigious Mr. Olympia title. Sergio Oliva competed in the Mr. Universe contest in London in 1971. Thus he was banned from the Mr. Olympia competition, that year held in Paris. Oliva lost to Bill Pearl in London, then flew to Paris to try to get a shot at Mr. Olympia. The ruling was not changed and Arnold Schwarzenegger won easily against a less than stellar field.

Chapter Six

Pumping Up

Nineteen seventy-two had gone well. Arnold prepared for the fall competitions and was again in top form. The 1972 Mr. Olympia was held in Essen, Germany, and, unlike 1971, all the top bodybuilders were there: Frank Zane, Franco Columbo, Serge Nubret, Sergio Oliva, and Arnold Schwarzenegger. Included in the audience was one spectator who had come specifically to see Arnold. Gustav Schwarzenegger watched as his son once again gained the Mr. Olympia title. This would be the last time that Arnold and Gustav would be together. Gustav died of a stroke on December 11, 1972. Arnold did not attend his father's funeral.

Why Arnold did not attend the funeral is still unclear. Many different explanations have been offered. In the movie *Pumping*

Pumping Up

Iron Arnold says he didn't go to the funeral because he was deep in training and there was nothing he could do. Actually, George Butler, one of the directors of the film and co-author of the book of the same name, had told the story to Arnold about someone else. Although they both knew it wasn't true they thought it was worth using in the film because it emphasized the level of commitment that bodybuilders have to their sport.

Butler's version of this story is that Arnold later told him that when his father died he was in Mexico doing an exhibition. Arnold went on vacation afterward, and no one could reach him. Reportedly Franco Columbo met Arnold at the airport when he returned to Los Angeles and told him of his father's death. By the time Arnold got the message, his father had already been buried. Arnold then took the next flight to Austria to be with his mother.

In a 1988 *Playboy* interview, Arnold tells yet another version. He claimed that he was in the hospital with a leg injury and was unable to travel to Austria. Over twenty years later it is not that important where the truth lies. What is important is how the stories surrounding Gustav's funeral point out Arnold's concern more with the impact of a statement than with the truth.

Prior to all this, on September 16, 1972, Arnold had been in New York at the Brooklyn Academy of Music for the Mr. America Competition. There he met the person who would probably do more to make Arnold a star than Joe Weider or anyone else. George Butler was there on a photographic assignment for *Oui* magazine. He was so impressed with Arnold Schwarzenegger that he decided almost immediately that Arnold should be the main focus of a book and then a movie on bodybuilders that he and Charles Gaines were planning to do. They had tentatively planned to call the book and the movie

Pumping Iron. Arnold might very well have become a star without the exposure of *Pumping Iron*, but it is doubtful that his star would have risen as meteorically.

Arnold's 1973 part in the movie *The Long Goodbye* is probably more like the type of part he would have gotten had he not been the focal point of *Pumping Iron*. *The Long Goodbye* is a Robert Altman film starring Elliott Gould as the private investigator Philip Marlowe. Raymond Chandler created the character and Marlowe was made famous by Humphrey Bogart in *The Big Sleep*. Arnold got the part through the recommendation of a friend who was working on the film. He once again used the stage name Arnold Strong. Arnold plays one of five hoods whose job it is to beat up Marlowe. Arnold has no lines in the movie, but does get to show off his muscles when one of the gangsters forces him to strip. Director Robert Altman reportedly said that he would never have forecast Arnold's success, but added that he thought Jack Nicholson wouldn't have made it either.

Nineteen seventy-three also brought Arnold his fourth straight Mr. Olympia title. Arnold Schwarzenegger was in the right place at the right time. His rise to dominance in the bodybuilding world coincided with the fitness craze that began in the early 1970s and continues today. And the fitness boom has a lot to do with the success of *Pumping Iron*, which in many ways should have been called *Pumping Arnold*.

Butler and Gaines had photographed and written about bodybuilding for a number of magazines when they came up with the idea for the book. To them, as to many, Arnold exemplified bodybuilding: He was the sport's biggest star. With Arnold as the center of the story they felt the chances of success for the book and the subsequent film were greater. Despite the eventual success of first the book and then the movie, there were problems along the way.

Doubleday, the original publisher of the book, did not feel the completed book was marketable and refused the manuscript. Butler, in his book, *Arnold Schwarzenegger: A Portrait*, writes that the editor of Doubleday wrote in the rejection letter that "no one in America will buy a book of pictures of these half-clothed men." Gaines and Butler went looking for another publisher. They finally convinced Simon & Schuster to publish the book. However, they received a much smaller advance payment than they had originally been offered.

When the book first came out, *The New York Times* refused to review it, feeling that its pictures of musclemen would only appeal to the homosexual community. Two months later *Pumping Iron* was on their bestseller list. The success of the book gave the two authors and their subject national exposure outside the limited world of bodybuilding. Butler has identified the November 1974 interview with Barbara Walters on NBC's "Today Show" as a pivotal moment in the growing popularity and acceptance of bodybuilding.

At first Walters was upset that Gaines and Butler had brought Arnold to the interview. As they talked in the preinterview before the show, Walters's opinion of Arnold began to change. She was impressed with his honest and straightforward responses to her questions. Arnold seemed to convince Walters and ultimately her national audience that there was more to bodybuilding than a bunch of oversized musclemen in love with their own bodies. It was a watershed moment for the sport and for Arnold. He had started bodybuilding at the age of fifteen and now, at twenty-seven, he had risen to the top of the field. In fact, he was raising the heights to which one could aspire in the bodybuilding world. From this point on his star would rise even faster.

The 1974 Mr. Olympia contest was held in New York in October at Madison Square Garden's Felt Forum. The place was packed with 5,000 enthusiastic fans. The four best bodybuilders in 1974 were at the competition. Arnold Schwarzenegger would be going for his fifth straight Mr. Olympia title. His major competition would come from Frank Zane, who had beaten Arnold the first time Arnold competed in America. Another tough competitor would be his best friend, Franco Columbo, who has been called the second-best bodybuilder of the era. Newcomer Lou Ferrigno, who would also make it big in Hollywood as David Banner's alter ego, the Incredible Hulk, would be another threat. Physically, Ferrigno was even bigger than Arnold. Yet as this was his first major professional competition, he lacked the polish and confidence it takes to be the very best in the sport. Again Arnold successfully defended his title.

It was at this time that the image of bodybuilding began to change. *Sports Illustrated* ran a lengthy article on bodybuilding in America that described Arnold's training techniques. Arnold trained in the original Gold's Gym in Santa Monica. People who are used to the fancy health clubs that have sprung up all over the country would find Gold's rather primitive. It is a nondescript building. Inside, weight machines and free weights are crowded everywhere you look. Training for an event generally starts six, eight, even twelve months in advance. Arnold's regimen had him working on his arms, thighs, calves, and abdominals on Mondays, Wednesdays, and Fridays. On Tuesdays, Thursdays, and Saturdays he worked on his chest, back, and shoulders, as well as his abdominals and calves. He would split his workouts, training for two hours in the morning and then

Pumping Up

returning to the gym for another hour in the late afternoon. In the course of a day Arnold would lift over forty tons of iron or 80,000 pounds. When they work out, bodybuilders are trying to achieve a condition known as "the pump." The pump occurs when the muscle is worked to the point that it requires additional oxygen. One can actually see and feel the blood rush to the muscles to supply the need.

Arnold is constantly asked for advice about weight training. He told Jack Mathews of the *Los Angeles Times*, "I love these guys who come into the gym and say 'Give me an exercise program, but I don't want to look like this' pointing to a picture of Mr. Universe. Don't worry, it's not likely."[1] Very few have the dedication that it takes to build a Mr. Universe body. And even fewer have the mental toughness to use that body to win.

After the 1974 Mr. Olympia competition, George Butler approached Arnold about making a documentary based on the book *Pumping Iron*. Arnold was at first reluctant. If he made the film with Butler he would have to train for and compete in the 1975 Mr. Olympia contest that would be held in Pretoria, South Africa.

Arnold had been seriously considering retiring from bodybuilding so that he could devote more time to his next career, acting. Charles Gaines had written a novel, *Stay Hungry*, which was nominated for a National Book Award. The book caught the attention of director Bob Rafelson, who decided to make a movie of the book. The story revolves around a love triangle between a bodybuilder who comes to Birmingham, Alabama, to compete, the woman who manages the gym where he trains, and a southern aristocratic man. Sally Fields and Jeff Bridges were cast to play the leads, all they needed was the bodybuilder. Gaines suggested Arnold Schwarzenegger.

Rafelson rejected the idea, but Gaines got him to agree to

meet Arnold. After the meeting, Rafelson reworked the part so it would be better suited for Arnold. Arnold was now scheduled to play Joe Santo, an Austrian bodybuilding champion who has come to the United States to compete. As part of the deal, Arnold agreed to take acting lessons. Eric Morris was recommended, and he agreed to give Arnold private lessons two to three hours a day, five days a week for twelve weeks.

There was one other adjustment that Rafelson wanted before the shooting of the movie was to begin. Two months before they were to start, he reportedly felt that a 240-pound Arnold was just too big. He was afraid he would dwarf the other stars. Arnold agreed to trim down for the movie and asked Rafelson what he wanted him to weigh. Rafelson suggested 210 pounds but doubted that Arnold could lose that much weight in just two months. Arnold bet him that he could. Just prior to shooting, Rafelson was in the gym with Arnold. After a sauna, Arnold jumped on the scale, which registered 209 pounds, much to Rafelson's astonishment.

While waiting for the shooting to start, Arnold spent a lot of time visiting the sets of other movies and TV shows. This gave him a better understanding of the moviemaking process. This was not to be another low budget *Hercules* flick—*Stay Hungry* was to be a major motion picture. Arnold started to put as much time and energy into acting as he had bodybuilding. For this movie there would be no Arnold Strong. This time he would do it his way and be Arnold Schwarzenegger, even though friends recommended he continue to use his stage name. There was one apparent downside to Arnold's growing involvement with Hollywood. Barbara Outland found the new Arnold not as desirable as the old. By mutual consent their long-standing relationship came to an end.

When the movie came out in 1976, it was greeted with

Pumping Up

mixed reviews. Most reviewers who mentioned Arnold, however, seemed to have good things to say about his performance. Jack Kroll of *Newsweek* wrote that Arnold was "surprisingly good as the muscle man with heart—and pectorals—of gold."[2] Arnold was nominated for a Golden Globe award for the best acting debut of 1976.

As soon as Arnold had finished shooting *Stay Hungry,* he was back in the gym training for Mr. Olympia. This included regaining the thirty pounds he had lost for his movie role as Joe Santo. But now the cameras were in the gym with him.

Despite the publication of *Pumping Iron*, Butler had a lot of difficulty getting financing for the film. Butler and a young filmmaker, Bill Beneson, made a fourteen-minute test film of an exhibition Arnold did in April 1974 in Holyoke, Massachusetts. Butler reports in his book, *Arnold Schwarzenegger: A Portrait*, that he showed the test film to a group of friends and potential investors in New York. At the viewing, one member of the audience stood up when the lights came on and said, "If you ever . . . put this oaf Arnold Schwarzenegger on the screen you'll be laughed off Forty-second Street." Apparently these New Yorkers didn't recognize a diamond in the rough. Somehow, Butler managed to find the money to shoot the film.

Pumping Iron follows a number of the contestants as they prepare for the 1975 Mr. Olympia. Arnold Schwarzenegger is obviously the most important bodybuilder in the film. It is not surprising at the end when he wins the title for an unprecedented sixth time. The film gives the viewer insight into a sport that had previously been relegated to a dark closet in the sporting world.

After they had finished shooting the film, Butler once again ran short of funding. In an effort to impress potential investors with the popularity of bodybuilding, Butler arranged for an exhibition by Arnold, Frank Zane, and Ed Corney. At first he thought he would rent a theater for the exhibition but that proved too costly. Butler came up with the idea of doing it in a museum. The Whitney Museum in New York City agreed to host the exhibition on February 25, 1976, and called it "Articulate Muscle—The Body as Art."

Butler felt that a less massive Arnold would be more appealing to his potential investors so he asked Arnold to slim down once again. This time Arnold lost thirty pounds within a few weeks. Although ticket sales were poor initially, by 7:30 on the night of the exhibition, 3,000 people had jammed themselves into the gallery to see Arnold and the other bodybuilders. It was so crowded that many of the investors, who had arrived stylishly late, never got inside the museum that night. The crowd was a bit unruly, reportedly interrupting the panel of art historians that the museum had assembled. They were trying to discuss the relationship between art and muscle. The audience let them know that they would prefer to see the live exhibition. Even though many of the investors never got to see Arnold, they were sufficiently impressed by the crowd that Butler finally got the money to finish *Pumping Iron.*

It seemed as though one thing just led to another for Arnold. As his ascendancy in bodybuilding had been inevitable, it appeared early on that the same would be true of his Hollywood career. As the reigning Mr. Olympia and the subject of Gaines and Butler's book, Arnold was invited onto the "Merv Griffin Show." Lucille Ball and her husband, producer Gary Morton, were watching and Lucy reportedly thought Arnold was charming.

After seeing him on the Griffin show, Lucy invited Arnold to be on her 1975 special, "Happy Anniversary and Goodbye." Arnold agreed and with the personal attention of Lucy had a role in a skit about one of Lucy's friends who needs to get in shape. Arnold plays the role of an Italian masseur. Arnold Schwarzenegger has credited Lucille Ball with giving him the exposure that got his acting career going.

At the end of the 1975 Mr. Olympia competition, he received the winner's trophy from his longtime idol Reg Park. Then Arnold Schwarzenegger officially announced his retirement from bodybuilding. This time he meant it. As he told the stunned audience of his plans, he promised not to desert bodybuilding even though he would no longer compete. Except for a controversial return from retirement for the 1980 Mr. Olympia in Sydney, Australia, he has been true to his word. Arnold has been one of the major forces in increasing the money available for the top bodybuilders. In partnership with Jim Lorimer, a Columbus, Ohio, businessman, they put on the Mr. Olympia competition for a number of years. The two men had been friends since Lorimer made the special plane arrangements for Arnold to get to the 1970 Pro Mr. World competition.

After Arnold announced his retirement in South Africa, he returned to California with the intention of pursuing his acting career. There is a story that has been reported in a number of places of Arnold's first attempts to get an agent. Supposedly these agents took one look at Arnold's massive body, heard his heavy Austrian accent, and wrote him off. They told him that he would never make it out in Hollywood. Arnold took this as a challenge and immediately signed up for voice lessons and more acting classes. He threw himself into the advancement of his dream as he had done at every other obstacle in his climb to the top. It was much like young Arnold searching for the sport he could be the best in the world at. He had to find his spot in Hollywood and then make the most of it.

Arnold Schwarzenegger

Well, now I'm in a $20 million movie [Conan]. I have the title role and the two same agents are killing themselves.

Hey, do you know what ten percent of a certain amount of money can add up to?

The agents were stupid. They didn't know whether or not I could act but already they said "no." To me it sounded like my father saying, "Let's see who's best?" I suppose I have competition in my heart, my head. But when I hear rejection, I am inspired to try to triumph.[3]

Chapter Seven

∎

In the Movies

▨　▨　▨　▨　▨　▨

By 1976 Arnold Schwarze-
negger was reportedly making over $200,000 a year from his
various business enterprises. Many people would have considered that an exceptional livelihood for a twenty-eight-year-old
retired bodybuilder. But Arnold was not one to rest on his accomplishments. He and Lorimer made the 1976 Mr. Olympia a
financial success for themselves and for the competitors.
Franco Columbo won the 1976 competition and Frank Zane
won the next three that Arnold and Lorimer produced. In that
time the prize money went from $1,000 to $50,000.

Arnold also went from living in an apartment in a building
he owned in Santa Monica, California, to driving a Mercedes

and parking it in front of his new $200,000 house in Santa Monica.

Arnold was also willing to give something back to the community. In 1974 Arnold visited the Terminal Island Prison to train with the inmates. Arnold felt that weight training would be a good outlet for some of the inmates' anger and negative energy. He devised a rehabilitative weight-training program, and then visited all the California prisons to promote it. He had gotten involved because he received a lot of letters from prisoners who wanted training tips.

The film *Pumping Iron* opened at New York's Plaza Theatre on January 18, 1977. This finally gave Arnold the opportunity to show himself as an unequaled self-promoter. Arnold Schwarzenegger became the darling of the "in crowd" in New York. A long list of celebrities attended the premiere. Arnold flew his mother over for it and made sure she knew at least one line of English: "I am Arnold's mother." Arnold was staying at the Park Lane Hotel, and only carrying hundred-dollar bills. Just prior to this Arnold had received the Golden Globe award for best acting debut for 1976 for his part in *Stay Hungry*. Suddenly, quite literally, everyone wanted Arnold Schwarzenegger.

Morley Safer did a "Sixty Minutes" segment on him entitled "Pumping Gold," which aired in the fall of 1977. Both Mercedes and BMW offered him a car. Austrian Airlines offered him a free ski trip for himself and fifty of his friends. Jamie Wyeth, a famous painter, painted a portrait of Arnold using Andy Warhol's studio. Warhol and Arnold became friends, and when Arnold had more money he started collecting Warhol artwork. Warhol may have assumed that this was Arnold's "fifteen minutes of fame," an expression that Warhol had originated. Little did anyone know that fifteen years later Arnold would be a bigger star and better known than any of the celebrities who were hanging out with him at this time.

Arnold and George Butler went to Europe to attend the Cannes Film Festival in 1977. They flew over early to do some traveling before the festival, and Arnold took Butler to meet many of his friends in Munich and elsewhere. One of the most poignant stories that Butler or anyone else tells about Arnold is about their visit to Arnold's hometown. Reportedly Arnold, after brashly taking Butler around his old haunts, rented a plain old Volkswagen for the drive to Thal. Arnold was no longer flashing hundred-dollar bills or putting on any bravado. In front of his relatives and friends in his hometown he reverted to a much simpler, quieter version of himself. This may be one of the few times that Arnold Schwarzenegger has let anyone outside his family see that side of him.

At Cannes, Arnold's notoriety continued. At one point a picture session on the beach with Arnold and the dancers from Paris's famous Crazy Horse Saloon was arranged. Arnold wore posing trunks and the women wore long summer dresses and wide-brimmed sun hats decorated with flowers. Reportedly 50,000 spectators turned out to see what was fast becoming the most famous set of muscles in the world.

One thing that did show through the sweat and the muscles of *Pumping Iron* was Arnold's star quality. Richard Schickel, in his review of the documentary, saw Arnold as "a cool, shrewd and boyish charmer, he exudes the easy confidence of a man who has always known he will be a star."[1]

The publishing world was also quick to jump on the Arnold Schwarzenegger bandwagon. *Arnold: The Education of a Bodybuilder* came out in 1977 written by Arnold Schwarzenegger and Douglas Kent Hall. As a combination bodybuilding autobiography and weight-training guide book, it was a runaway bestseller. Unlike most authors, though, Arnold was not satisfied with having been involved in the writing of the book. He took an active part in the selling of the book as well. He not only did the usual promotional tours, but went a step farther than most authors when he met with the salespeople Simon & Schuster had assigned to market his book.

On one promotional trip to Birmingham, Alabama, Arnold was met at the airport by a publicist and a limo. As he was waiting for his luggage he noticed a group of writers, including best-selling novelists John Barth and Eudora Welty, boarding a bus to go to a writer's conference. Arnold was startled by the difference between the way he was being treated and the way those writers were being treated. He wanted to speak at their conference about how to promote books and get the red carpet treatment.

One thing Arnold never lost sight of while he hyped himself was his allegiance to bodybuilding. He wanted to legitimize the sport of bodybuilding so that it would get the kind of attention from the media and the general public that he felt it deserved. In reading *Arnold: The Education of a Bodybuilder,* you realize Arnold's dedication and enthusiasm. The book was dedicated to his mother and Butler and Gaines. Of the two *Pumping Iron* collaborators, Arnold wrote that their "genuine enthusiasm, energy and talent changed the sport of bodybuilding and . . . I am honored to count [them] among my closest friends."

Although since his Munich days Arnold has never lacked for the attention of women, he has had only a few serious relationships. Barbara Outland can be considered the first; the second rolled into his life in 1977. Arnold met Sue Moray, a twenty-five-year-old athletic blond, as she rollerskated along Venice Beach, California, in July 1977. After a brief conversation, Arnold asked her for her phone number and they were soon living together in what has been referred to as an "open relationship." Arnold reportedly helped Sue get a job as a hair stylist at a hair salon near Gold's Gym, where he still worked out on a regular basis.

Later that same summer, in August 1977, Arnold first met the woman he would later marry. The publicist for the film *Pumping Iron* got Arnold an invitation to the Robert F. Kennedy Tennis Tournament that was being held at Forest Hills, New York. At the tournament, Arnold met many Kennedy family members, including Maria Shriver. Arnold was invited to come for the weekend to the Kennedy family compound at Hyannis Port, on Cape Cod, Massachusetts.

Although the invitation came from Maria Shriver and her brother Bobby, Arnold spent time with many family members. He played tennis with Sargent Shriver, Maria's dad, and went boating with Maria's mother, Eunice Kennedy Shriver. Arnold was also able to converse in his native German with Sargent Shriver and Maria's uncle, Sen. Ted Kennedy.

Maria is eight years younger than Arnold and had just graduated from Georgetown University with a B.A. in American Studies. Although she had been exposed to politics her whole life, she felt that her future was in journalism. In 1972, when she was sixteen, she had traveled with her father as he ran as the vice presidential candidate with George McGovern. Rather than spending her time with the political insiders, she found herself attracted to the members of the press who were traveling with her father. It was then that she got the idea to go into journalism. Like her future husband, Maria was willing and able to put in the hard work to make it to the top echelons of her career. And like Arnold, she has the charisma that is necessary to be successful in front of the cameras, whether they be TV news cameras or motion picture cameras.

Arnold Schwarzenegger

One interesting offshoot of Arnold's visit to Hyannis Port was the beginning of his involvement with the Special Olympics. Eunice Kennedy Shriver is very active in the Special Olympics, an organization that gives people with mental and physical handicaps the opportunity to compete in athletic competitions. Shortly after meeting Eunice, Arnold became the honorary weight-lifting coach for the Special Olympics, a post he continues to hold. Arnold helped develop a weight-lifting program for Special Olympians. He traveled around the country holding demonstrations and raising money to buy weight-lifting equipment for the Special Olympics. Arnold feels that Special Olympians enjoy weight lifting because it is something anyone can succeed at. Improvement is easily measured when you can lift more weight than when you started.

Maria tried to find a job in New York City, without any luck. She landed a job in Philadelphia as a newswriter and producer for KYW-TV. Maria stayed in Philadelphia for about a year and then moved to WJZ-TV in Baltimore, Maryland. Arnold would see Maria when various activities brought him to the East Coast. Arnold began changing his image at this time. He began having his suits custom-made for his muscular body, and he started to dress more like a preppy and less like a California muscleman.

As much as Arnold wanted to be in the movies, he was being selective. He made the right choice when he turned down an opportunity to play a muscleman in the 1978 Mae West movie *Sextette*: The movie was a bomb. Arnold also turned down $200,000 to do a commercial for a tire company. In the commercial Arnold was slated to say that he had worked fifteen years to get his muscles but wasn't half as strong as the tires.

In the fall of 1978, Arnold got another shot at the movies. He was cast as the handsome but shy stranger in *The Villain*, a

In the Movies

Western comedy that starred Ann-Margret and Kirk Douglas. The movie was directed by former stuntman Hal Needham, who had directed the Burt Reynolds hits *Smokey and the Bandit* and *Hooper*. Needham has said that Arnold was easy to work with and fun to be around. Arnold received $275,000 for his role in the movie. Although Carlos Clarens wrote in *Film Comment* that Arnold proved he could be "funny and spirited on film," *The Villain* was a bust at the box office.[2]

For Christmas 1978, Arnold went skiing in Europe, accompanied by Maria Shriver. Maria's mother had wanted her to join the family on a trip to Africa, but Maria opted for the ski trip to Austria that continued with a trip to Hawaii. Then she and Arnold returned to their work on opposite coasts of the United States. Their long-distance relationship went on, and Maria was again Arnold's traveling companion when he attended the 1979 Cannes Film Festival to promote *The Villain*.

During this time he got a guest spot on the hit TV series "The Streets of San Francisco." Arnold was cast as a European bodybuilder who had moved to the United States. The character turned out to be the villain who killed any woman who refused his advances.

The increasing popularity of bodybuilding gave Arnold another opportunity to increase his public exposure. CBS hired Arnold as an expert commentator to assist them in their coverage of the 1979 Mr. Olympia contest held in Columbus, Ohio. He was also the commentator for the 1980 Miss Olympia contest held in Philadelphia. When Arnold asked Frank Zane how it felt to win his third Mr. Olympia in a row, Zane replied that it felt even better than the time he beat Arnold.

Arnold's second book, *Arnold's Body Shaping for Women,* came out in 1979. Again written with Douglas Kent Hall, this book evolved from Arnold's discovery that American women, unlike European women, rarely worked out with weights. During his travels many women had asked him questions about their using weights. The book introduces readers to using weights to improve their overall conditioning.

In Hollywood, Arnold was still being typecast as a bodybuilder. His next role was Mickey Hargitay, Jayne Mansfield's second husband, in the made-for-TV movie *The Jayne Mansfield Story*. Hargitay had been the 1956 NABBA Mr. Universe. Loni Anderson starred as Jayne Mansfield, a megastar of the 1950s whose career came to an abrupt end when she died in a drunk-driving accident at 36. Mansfield had become another victim of the abuses of Hollywood, and Arnold was impressed by the tragedy of her story. He realized just how vicious the movie business could be.

But that's not all he learned about "the business" while working on *Mansfield*: "I learned that you have to establish yourself in an area where there is no one else. Then you have to create a need for yourself." Then what happens is that "all of a sudden, it's too late for them to do anything about it. And *they* have to come to *you,* because you have what they want."[3]

Chapter Eight

The Barbarian

In his next film Arnold found the place where he could excel. The title role of *Conan the Barbarian* defined Arnold's place at the box office. With the exception of the movie *Twins,* from this point forward there would be a little of the "Barbarian" in any of Arnold's pictures. Wherever his character is, there is a similarity that all Schwarzenegger fans have come to expect, whether on Mars or the mean streets of Chicago, in the future or the distant past. All Arnold's characters are good guys—with the exception of the first Terminator—but they willingly mete out their own uniquely violent form of justice. There are no rules when you are eliminating the bad guys.

Arnold almost didn't get the part of Conan. When Arnold

was being interviewed by producer Dino De Laurentiis in 1978 to play Flash Gordon he made a critical error. Arnold had walked into De Laurentiis's office and was amazed that such a small man sat behind such a large ornate desk. Arnold asked De Laurentiis why he needed such a large desk. De Laurentiis was deeply offended. The interview lasted less than two minutes, and Arnold didn't get that part. De Laurentiis didn't want to give him the part of Conan either. However, John Milius, the director, was convinced that Arnold was the only one who could play Conan. Fortunately for Arnold, and movie fans everywhere, Milius prevailed. De Laurentiis signed Arnold to a deal that called for five pictures. He also bought $40,000 worth of weight-lifting equipment that traveled with Arnold so that he could maintain his physical form for the movie.

John Milius had a long list of movie credits before he got to *Conan.* He had worked on *Dirty Harry,* he wrote the script for *Magnum Force* and co-wrote the scripts for *Jeremiah Johnson* and *Apocalypse Now.* His credits as a director included *Dillinger* and *The Wind and the Lion.* Milius was the driving force behind the Conan movie. He and Oliver Stone (*Born on the Fourth of July* and *JFK*) wrote the script for *Conan the Barbarian.* They adapted it from a series of stories that had been written in the 1930s by Robert E. Howard. In the 1960s Conan became very popular as the stories were published in book form and used as comic book material. The popularity of the Conan stories, and later the movies, are part of the growth of the whole genre known as sword and sorcery.

The story line that Milius and Stone came up with starts out with a young Conan witnessing the destruction of his home village and the murder of his parents at the hands of Thulsa Doom (played by James Earl Jones). The young Conan is captured and enslaved to work on the Wheel of Pain. As the boy grows into a man he is taken from the slave pits to be trained as a gladiator. He eventually wins his freedom, and the now-powerful Conan sets out to seek revenge for the deaths of his parents.

Along the way he teams up with a thief, a wizard, and Valeria, a woman warrior who is also his love interest (played by Sandahl Bergman). The group heads out to steal the Eye of the Serpent, a huge red jewel, from the snake tower. They are then asked by King Osric (played by Max Von Sydow) to rescue his daughter from Thulsa Doom. The small band is ultimately successful. Conan gets his revenge by beheading Thulsa Doom and destroying the snake cult. During their escape, however, Valeria is killed.

The most difficult character to cast was Conan. There were very few people in the world who had the body that fit the image of Conan that had appeared on the cover of magazines and books, and throughout the pages of Conan comic books. In fact, in Milius's mind there was only one person who could play the part. That was the man with the greatest body in the world, Arnold Schwarzenegger.

Arnold realized from the beginning of the project that this might be just the movie he needed to forward his plan and carve himself a place in the Hollywood world. Arnold was willing to do just about anything to make Conan a success. He continued the acting lessons he had been taking off and on since *Stay Hungry*. He spent the year prior to the beginning of filming studying the martial arts and learning how to fight with a broadsword while wearing armor. Arnold would often work out with costar Sandahl Bergman so they could practice their sword fighting. He also found himself seriously training in the gym to get his body in top form for the part. Part of the success of *Conan* depended upon the movie projecting a Conan who fit the romanticized artwork that the readers of sword and sorcery books and comic books had come to expect. This would be Arnold's first starring role in a major Hollywood production, and he wanted every muscle rippling so that he would fulfill the expectations of the audience.

While all the preparations for *Conan* were going on, Arnold's friends in the gym were getting ready for the 1980 Mr. Olympia contest to be held in Sydney, Australia. Some of the bodybuilders thought that Arnold was planning to come out of retirement and compete. It made many of them very nervous to think that they would once more have to contend with the greatest bodybuilder ever. Arnold told most people that he was just getting in shape for the role of Conan. He would be going to Sydney only as a commentator for the television coverage. Some believed him, but others weren't convinced.

The skeptics were justified. Arnold created a furor at the 1980 Mr. Olympia contest by showing up and announcing that he would be a contestant. Many of the bodybuilders were extremely upset that Arnold was allowed to compete at the last minute. No doubt they were jealous of Arnold and felt that he was now rich and famous and, in their minds, had nothing to gain by competing.

Arnold won the 1980 Mr. Olympia contest, much to the dismay of his fellow competitors. There were protests over the results and accusations that it was rigged as five of the seven judges were good friends of Arnold's. Yet other competitors believed that Arnold deserved the victory. By not declaring his intentions and waiting until he was in Sydney to announce that he would compete, Arnold did what he had done before. He beat his competition before the contest began. He created such a storm of controversy that he seemed to be the only one focused on the contest. Arnold admitted that physically he was only about ninety percent of what he had been at his peak. Mentally, however, he was at one hundred percent, and that was where the competition was won.

The 1980 Mr. Olympia was Arnold's last bodybuilding competition. Although he won, he found that bodybuilding wasn't as satisfying as it had once been. He had achieved everything that bodybuilding could offer him, including wealth and fame. It was time to move on.

Conan the Barbarian was filmed in Spain for six months. Right from the beginning, Milius had a problem. In most movies, the stars use doubles to do the more dangerous stunts. It was almost impossible to find a stand-in who would have the size and muscles to pass for Arnold. The only solution was to have Arnold do all but a few of his own stunts.

Arnold readily agreed to this and rehearsed his stunts carefully. Even with the practice and the precautions that were taken, there was still risk involved. For one stunt, where Conan is attacked by wolves, Arnold practiced for a week with dogs to get over his fear of vicious animals. When it was time to shoot the scene, the wolves were released too early. Arnold was still climbing up onto a pile of rocks and the wolves got hold of him and knocked him down. Arnold fell ten feet and landed on his back. The fall caused a gash in his back that required stitches. This was the first scene that was shot. Milius reportedly told Arnold that now he knew what working on the film would be like. In the rest of the shooting, Arnold would have to jump from a forty-foot-high tower, work with huge snakes, get kicked by a camel, run over by horses, cut by swords, and thrown over by an elephant. Hardly a day went by when Arnold wasn't cut or bruised. The only time he was clean was when he was asleep.

In addition to the cuts, bruises, dirt, and treacherous stunts,

Arnold Schwarzenegger

Arnold had to put up with the extremes of climate. The company moved to a variety of locations throughout Spain. The filming started with Arnold out in the snow in a loincloth and finished in sweltering, mosquito-infested heat. Milius wanted the film to be as realistic as possible, to the point of not allowing lightweight replica weapons. The sword that Arnold wields as Conan weighs over ten pounds. The movie begins with a line from the philosopher Nietzsche, "That which does not kill us makes us stronger." This was true for the character as well as the actor. Despite many negative reviews, *Conan the Barbarian* was all that Arnold could have hoped it would be.

The movie had cost $19 million to make and when it was released on May 14, 1982, it was an instant success. *Conan* grossed $9.6 million in its first weekend and has grossed more than $100 million worldwide. Only a few of the reviewers who saw the movie understood what it offered. It is the same thing that all fantasies have to offer: an escape to a time and place where good wins and muscles matter. Those who went to see Conan wield his sword like a barbarian in revenge for the deaths of his parents were not disappointed. Stallone, Eastwood, Ford, and Norris had all found their special niches in the area of action-adventure movies. Now Arnold Schwarzenegger was poised to do the same.

Chapter Nine

Destroyer to Terminator

After the filming of *Conan the Barbarian,* Arnold's third book came out. *Arnold's Bodybuilding for Men,* coauthored by Bill Dobbins, was very successful. The book provides exercises for men to get into shape and to stay in shape using weights. It is directed at men in general but also gives aspiring bodybuilders some of Arnold's expert knowledge on diet and specialized training. In addition, Arnold included a section on weight lifting for teens. He is adamant that preteens are not yet ready for weight training and should train only with the weight of their bodies, such as chin-ups, sit-ups, and push-ups. Arnold also recommends running, bicycling, and swimming as activities that would be good exercises for preteens and others who want to get into shape.

During this time, Arnold and Maria continued to see each other when they could. In 1981 Maria moved to California, hoping to transfer from producing to reporting. Her ultimate goal was to become an anchorwoman. When Maria arrived on the West Coast, she went to see an agent to find representation. Reportedly, the agent told her she looked terrible and that he wouldn't even consider representing her. He told her she needed to lose weight and get herself pulled together.

Maria was at first stunned and then realized that the agent was right. She lost weight and took voice lessons to improve her diction. She also worked on being able to develop thoughts and questions within the immediate framework of an interview. As a producer she had had the luxury of thinking things through in advance. If she was to make it in front of the camera she would have to learn to think and react quickly during an interview. When she was ready, Maria returned to the same agent, who immediately signed on to represent her.

As Arnold's career in the movies expanded, so did Maria's career in TV journalism. For the first two years she was on the West Coast she was a national correspondent for Group W's "PM Magazine." In 1983 she became the West Coast reporter for the CBS "Morning News."

Arnold's next career move was to make a sequel to *Conan the Barbarian. Conan the Destroyer,* as one reviewer put it, was much closer to the Conan of the comic books. A change in directors also changed the direction in which the character traveled. Milius was replaced on this project by Richard Fleischer, a director with many credits, but probably best known for the 1954 Disney hit *20,000 Leagues Under the Sea.*

Conan the Destroyer was filmed in Mexico starting in November 1983. Fleischer was the first director to allow Arnold's wry comic sense to be seen. Sequels often have difficulty living

One of Arnold's early film roles cast him as the ferocious
warrior Conan the Destroyer. His huge muscles, created by
years of bodybuilding, made him perfect for the part. (©*1984
Universal City Studios, Inc.*)

Arnold played a less serious role when he teamed up with the comical Danny DeVito, who played his long-lost brother, in *Twins*. (©*1988 Universal City Studios, Inc.*)

Arnold thinks physical activity is important for American children. Former President Bush agreed and Arnold became the popular spokesman for the President's Council on Physical Fitness and Sports. (*The President's Council on Physical Fitness and Sports*)

Arnold appears very pleased with TV news anchor and bride
Maria Shriver on their wedding day. (*UPI/Bettmann*)

Arnold uses his popularity and influence in films like
Kindergarten Cop to encourage children to exercise regularly.
(©1990 Universal City Studios, Inc.)

A man of Arnold's size stands out in any crowd, but that's especially true in the principal's office in *Kindergarten Cop*. (©*1990 Universal City Studios, Inc.*)

He's back. In *Terminator 2*, Arnold returned as a good guy, to save the world from destruction. (©*1991 Carolco*)

Arnold kept his good guy image and showed moviegoers that even tough guys have a soft side when he teamed with newcomer Austin O'Brien in *Last Action Hero*. (©*1992 Columbia Pictures Industries, Inc.*)

up to originals, and this is true of *The Destroyer.* The main weakness with the second *Conan* movie was the premise of the adventure. In *The Barbarian,* Conan is clearly motivated by revenge, an emotion that we can all relate to. In *The Destroyer,* Conan is on a quest to help the evil Queen Taramis. In exchange for Conan's help, Taramis says she will bring Valeria, who had died at the end of *The Barbarian,* back to life. Conan agrees to the terms and sets out on his quest with the Princess Jehenna who is to retrieve a magic key and a jewel-encrusted horn. They are accompanied by a thief, a wizard, Zula (an imposing woman warrior played by Grace Jones), and Princess Jehenna's bodyguard Bombaata, played by basketball great, seven-foot-two-inch Wilt Chamberlain. Bombaata has secret instructions to kill Conan once the quest is accomplished. It is hard for the audience to believe that the grief-stricken Conan could be taken in by Queen Taramis and a promise she never intended to keep.

Despite the weakness of the plot, the action and special effects of *The Destroyer* satisfied the audience's cravings for more Conan. In the final scene Conan rescues the about-to-be-sacrificed Princess Jehenna and battles the recently reawakened evil demon Dagoth. It is an exciting scene. Many in the audience wonder if Conan will be able to defeat such a powerful adversary. In the end, good triumphs, Princess Jehenna is saved and becomes the new queen, rewarding all who had helped her. She obviously wishes to share her throne with Conan but he still grieves for the lost Valeria and leaves to seek further adventures.

Conan the Destroyer proved once again that many who make their living reviewing movies don't really understand the vast array of interests of the movie-going public. *Conan the Destroyer* had worldwide grosses that were comparable to

Conan the Barbarian. Many loyal fans no doubt hoped that there would be more Conan films, just as there had been a whole series of Hercules movies that Arnold and his generation had watched. That was not to be the case. Some have speculated that had Arnold continued to make Conan movies, he would have never been able to escape the character and achieve the immense success he now enjoys.

After filming *Conan the Destroyer,* Arnold achieved a milestone of another type. On September 16, 1983, along with two thousand other people, Arnold Schwarzenegger became an American citizen. Arnold dressed in a blue-and-white striped suit and wore a red tie for the swearing-in ceremony. In his hand he carried a small American flag. Afterward he turned to the assembled journalists and said, "I always believe in shooting for the top, and becoming an American is like becoming a member of the winning team."[1] One unusual aspect of Arnold's new citizenship was that he maintained, with help from friends in Austria, his Austrian citizenship.

Arnold Schwarzenegger was living proof that the American dream was still alive. Anyone willing to work hard enough, with a little luck and the right physical and mental attributes, can still start with nothing and achieve immense success. Arnold had been the world's greatest bodybuilder; he invested wisely in real estate; amassed a substantial fortune; and had been in eight films. At this point, Arnold could have retired comfortably and never worked again, but that was not what he was looking for. Before long Arnold Schwarzenegger would redefine the term "megastar."

In Arnold's next movie he escaped the image of beefcake muscleman. As those who had known him as the world's top bodybuilder already knew, there is much, much more to Arnold than just rippling muscles. This would become obvious when Arnold Schwarzenegger became *The Terminator.*

Many consider this Arnold's best film. He plays a time-traveling cyborg that is sent back to the twentieth century. His mission is to kill a woman, whose yet-to-be-born son will be the leader of a rebellion against the machines that control the post-nuclear holocaust future. At the very least, *The Terminator* is one of the films against which all other science-fiction thrillers are judged.

Originally, director James Cameron, who co-wrote the script with the film's producer Gale Anne Hurd, had pictured the Terminator as able to fit into a crowd. He definitely did not have Arnold Schwarzenegger in mind. Arnold went to see Cameron about playing the role of Kyle Reese, the human who is sent back to warn and protect the Terminator's target, Sarah Connor. But as he read the script, Arnold became intrigued with the role of the part-human, part-machine cyborg. The script was then reworked to fit the Terminator that Arnold brought before the cameras. The Terminator has only fourteen lines in the movie, including the now famous "I'll be back." This was not a subtle infiltration unit. Arnold's Terminator was a cyborg to be reckoned with.

Arnold is so convincing as the Terminator that no one who sees the movie is surprised when the human flesh is damaged and the machine underneath is revealed. Cameron intended the movie to appeal to different segments of the movie audience in different ways. On one level the movie addresses the action-adventure-loving audience that wants chase scenes, explosions, and shoot-outs. On another level, it forces those who wish to do so to think about man's relationship with the machines that become more sophisticated every day. Cameron's intention was to make people think about what the future could be like if evil ever prevails.

Unlike the Conan movies, for the most part the critics liked *The Terminator* when it was released in the fall of 1984. "*The Terminator* made Arnold a star by turning all his liabilities into perverse virtues: The movie acknowledged his lumbering, robotic quality, and used it as a comic counterpoint to the snappy, quick-witted narrative."[2] Even Maria Shriver, who had disliked the violence in the *Conan* movies, liked *The Terminator*. For some moviegoers it is the only Arnold Schwarzenegger movie they like.

The Terminator was one of the biggest hits of 1984, grossing over $100 million worldwide. Arnold felt that its success would double his price for his next movie. *Time* magazine chose it as one of the ten best films of the year, and Arnold was voted "International Star of 1984" by the National Association of Theatre Owners. Arnold seemed to know what moviegoers wanted and was seen as "the most quintessential of American movie stars. Why? Because self-reinvention is what America is ultimately about, and Schwarzenegger's movie career amounts to astute reinvention—in constant public view."[3]

Chapter Ten

Taking Command

Before *The Terminator* was released, Arnold had already begun filming his next movie. Dino De Laurentiis had convinced Arnold to once again play a sword-wielding character in a sword-and-sorcery movie. This time, however, he would be playing backup sword to newcomer Brigitte Nielsen. With a change of hair color, Nielsen attempted to play the lead role in the movie, *Red Sonja*.

Richard Fleischer was again called upon to direct and the cast arrived at Pontini Studios in Rome on September 24, 1984, to begin shooting. Nielsen might have been more convincing as the Amazonian Sonja had she spent some time before the movie pumping up with Arnold. When watching the movie it is hard to believe that her willowy arms can even lift the sword.

Arnold Schwarzenegger

To say nothing about becoming a sword master capable of decapitating a foe with one swing of her two-handed broadsword. Arnold had been included in the cast so that his name would draw an audience. Even the most loyal *Conan* fans were disappointed by this movie. Ernie Reyes, Jr., who plays the pint-size child prince of a destroyed land, got all the best lines. It was obviously a low budget attempt to cash in on the success of the *Conan* movies and it failed.

Arnold usually is one of the most active promoters of anything he is involved in. However, even Arnold ignored *Red Sonja*. He reportedly told De Laurentiis that he was through making *Conan*-style movies because De Laurentiis wasn't fully committed to doing it right. De Laurentiis was in agreement. In addition to all the movie's shortcomings, the whole concept of *Red Sonja* neglected a major point about sword-and-sorcery viewers. The core of the audience for this type of movie is composed of young males who want to see Conan defeating evil. They don't want to watch an unconvincing redheaded woman do the fighting. Fortunately for Arnold, *Red Sonja* was quickly forgotten as he rode the wave of success of *The Terminator* and the action-adventure movies that followed.

Arnold had made a transition from sword-wielding barbarian to evil cyborg from the future. In his next movie, *Commando*, his role changes again and he portrays a retired Special Forces colonel, John Matrix. His daughter is kidnaped by a group of renegade Special Forces soldiers. These soldiers are planning to launch a war in Latin America from an island off California. They want Matrix to assassinate the president of the country they are fighting so they can regain it for a deposed dictator. Matrix has the choice of going along with the kidnappers or taking matters into his own hands. From the first chase scene to the last explosion, there is no doubt in anyone's mind that

Taking Command

Col. John Matrix will do all that he can to save his daughter, Jenny. She is played by Alyssa Milano, best known for her role as Tony's daughter on the TV series *Who's the Boss*. Arnold is assisted in his one-man rampage by Rae Dawn Chong. Chong provides some welcome comic relief to the movie. The comedy serves to set this movie apart from other action-adventure films.

Arnold felt that humor would add to the appeal of the movie. When not in front of the cameras, Arnold is a funny man who enjoys practical jokes. In fact, the producer of *Commando*, Joel Silver, was quoted as saying that he had expected Arnold "to be a quiet, stoic, big construction of a guy, and he's like one of the Three Stooges."[1] Sometimes, however, Arnold can get a little carried away with what he thinks will be funny in his movies. He wanted to put a gag into *Commando* where he hacked off the arm of one of his adversaries. When the mutilated villain started to scream, Arnold would hit him over the head with his own arm to shut him up. Then Arnold would walk away still holding on to the arm like a club. Moments later he would realize he was still carrying the arm and would discard it. The studio executives at Twentieth Century Fox vetoed the idea. We will never know if the audience would have thought it was funny or just too much.

During the filming of *Commando*, the force of Arnold's personality was felt by the other members of the production company. By the time they had completed the movie, many of the company had begun weight training with Arnold's encouragement and insistence that it would do them good. And all the stunt men were copying another one of Arnold's trademark habits: They were all smoking cigars. In fact, for the first time, Arnold is seen smoking a cigar in the movies. Cigars are one of his few indulgences in life and he likes big twenty-five-dollar-apiece Cuban cigars. He has stated that he likes big cigars because the little ones only last half an hour.

Commando made one thing obvious: The success of *The Terminator* was not a fluke. Arnold was now a star to be reckoned with, and he has put together an unprecedented string of successful movies. But 1985 was a milestone year in other ways as well.

On August 10, 1985, Arnold Schwarzenegger and Maria Shriver publicly announced their engagement. Arnold had carried the engagement ring around for six months waiting for just the right time to ask Maria to marry him. They had been on vacation in Hawaii but proposing on the beach in Hawaii seemed too much of a cliché, so he kept the ring in his pocket. Later that summer, Arnold and Maria were visiting Austria and Arnold was showing her around his hometown. As they passed the lake where Arnold had learned to swim as a child, he suggested that they go rowing. While out in the boat, Arnold pulled the ring out and proposed. Maria at first wasn't sure that he was serious, but when she realized that he was, she said yes.

Three weeks after they announced their engagement, Maria was offered the job opportunity that she had been waiting for. CBS offered her the position of co-anchor on the CBS "Morning News." Phyllis George had resigned after only nine months and Maria was excited about finally getting a shot at an anchor spot. There was, however, one major problem with the job. If she took the position, she would have to work in New York while Arnold remained in California. The recently engaged couple talked over the prospects of living once again on opposite coasts. Arnold was supportive of Maria's career goals. On September 2, 1985, Maria took over from Phyllis George, filling the seat next to Forrest Sawyer.

While in New York, Maria lived in a single hotel room fifteen blocks from the CBS building. She got up at 3:00 A.M. to be ready to go on the air live at 7:00 A.M. Every Friday, Maria would hop on a plane and fly off to be with Arnold. She would either join him in California or, if he was working on a picture, she would join him on location.

In anticipation of their wedding, Arnold and Maria looked for a new house in California. They found a Spanish-style estate that seemed perfect for them. It has seven bedrooms, four bathrooms, a swimming pool, tennis court, two acres of gardens with a stream, and a gym. The house reportedly cost $3 million.

Unlike many stars, the garages at the Schwarzenegger house were not filled with exotic sports cars. Arnold's favorite car was a 1957 Cadillac Eldorado Biarritz convertible, apparently because of its size. Arnold wasn't comfortable in sports cars. He liked the Eldorado because it would hold six passengers and it reminded him of the cars that he associated with the United States when he was growing up in Austria. He also had a Harley Davidson motorcycle and a Jeep that he had customized with a bigger engine and bigger tires.

The new house also contained Arnold's art collection. Joe Weider had introduced Arnold to art collecting years before. Weider is a fanatical collector and Arnold would go with him to auctions and shows. Arnold studied the literature that the various auction houses published, and started by collecting works by Chagall and Miro. He also likes Rauschenberg but in 1985 he had only one Rauschenberg print. Arnold also likes the sports paintings of Leroy Neiman, who did a full-body portrait of Arnold.

Chapter Eleven

Making Some Deals

$\mathbf{O}$n November 1, 1985, filming began on *Raw Deal,* Arnold's fourth movie to be produced by Dino De Laurentiis. Arnold played Kaminsky, who had been thrown out of the FBI on false charges. Now languishing as a small-town police chief, he is recruited by his former boss Harry Shannon (played by Darren McGavin) to infiltrate the Chicago mob. Shannon wants revenge—his son was murdered by the mobsters. Kaminsky fakes his own death to escape his small-town job and alcoholic wife. He arrives in Chicago as a minor criminal, a false identity arranged for him by Shannon.

Again Arnold has mixed the serious action-adventure genre with his own brand of comedy. Early in the movie Kaminsky comes home to his drunk wife. She explodes with anger and throws the cake she is decorating at him, and Kaminsky delivers one of his classic one-liners, "You shouldn't drink and bake." Despite the violence and Kaminsky's sometimes unethical practices of rubbing out the bad guys, the viewers are always rooting for him. Throughout the movie, he is a champion of the good guys. Even when Monique, played by Kathryn Harrold, tries to seduce Kaminsky, he remains loyal to his wife. A lesser man might have given in. Kaminsky is really Conan the Barbarian in a suit, cleaning up the streets of Chicago just as John Wayne cleaned up the streets of the West. It is good triumphing over evil that has ensured, in part, the success of *Raw Deal* and all of Arnold's movies.

When Arnold had finished filming *Raw Deal,* he moved on to what was to be one of the biggest deals of his life: He and Maria set their wedding date. They were married at 11:00 A.M. on April 26, 1986, at St. Francis Xavier's Roman Catholic Church in Hyannis, Massachusetts, with 450 guests in attendance. It was a star-studded event. Caroline Kennedy, Maria's cousin and daughter of the late president John F. Kennedy, was the maid of honor. The twelve bridesmaids included the sister of Queen Noor of Jordan, Alexa Halaby, as well as other of Maria's cousins. Maria's dress was designed by Marc Bohan of Christian Dior and was made of white satin edged with pearls, and had an eleven-foot train.

Security around the Kennedy family is understandably tight. When you add to them a guest list that included Hollywood and New York celebrities such as Grace Jones, Susan Saint James, Andy Williams, Barbara Walters, Tom Brokaw, Diane Sawyer, Oprah Winfrey, Forrest Sawyer, and a host of others, extraordinary measures needed to be taken. The entire eighty-five-person Barnstable County police department was on duty for the weekend. The guests were given small gold buttons that identified them for the police. One hundred rooms were reserved for wedding guests at the nearby Dunfy's Hyannis Hotel, and the hotel hired twenty extra security guards for the weekend. Although 450 guests may seem like a large wedding by some standards, it was a small and guarded list of people who received invitations. The Kennedy relatives alone accounted for over one hundred of the guests.

Arnold was in Puerta Vallarta, Mexico, filming *Predator* while the final preparations for the wedding were made. He flew in from Mexico on the Friday afternoon before the wedding. He then attended the rehearsal dinner hosted by his mother, Aurelia Schwarzenegger, at the Hyannisport Yacht Club. Arnold wore a formal Tyrolean outfit to the rehearsal dinner. Wiener schnitzel and Sacher torte, two traditional Austrian dishes, were served along with lobster and strawberry shortcake. Arnold referred to the meal as an "Austrian clambake." For his part, Arnold had Franco Columbo, his longtime friend and bodybuilding partner, as his best man. Among the twelve ushers were Arnold's cousin Karl Schwarzenegger, his nephew Patrick Knapp, Jim Lorimer, the Ohio businessmen who had helped Arnold promote bodybuilding, and Maria's four brothers.

The ceremony the next day lasted seventy-five minutes. Then they all went back to the Kennedy compound where two huge white tents had been set up for the reception. Peter Duchin's seven-piece band was flown in from New York and played everything from Cole Porter to the Rolling Stones. The guests were served oysters on the half shell, cold lobster, and chicken breasts with a champagne sauce. The wedding cake was a replica of the one that Maria's parents had at their wedding. It was seven feet tall, had eight tiers of carrot and pound cake covered with butter cream frosting, and weighed 425 pounds. Ex-

Making Some Deals

Olympian Donna De Varrona caught Maria's bouquet and Forrest Sawyer caught the bride's garter. Then the bride and groom headed off to their secret honeymoon location, later reported to be the St. James Club Hotel in Antigua.

Maria had not announced to her viewers that she was getting married that weekend and had only said that she would be away for a few days. Arnold had a film crew waiting in Mexico, so their honeymoon lasted only a few days before they both had to be back at work thousands of miles apart.

The newlyweds continued their bicoastal marriage until September 1986 when CBS canceled its morning news show and fired Maria Shriver and Forrest Sawyer. At the time Maria felt betrayed by the network for whom she had been working eighteen hours a day, giving everything she had to her job. In the June 1992 issue of *McCall's,* Maria is quoted as saying, "They pulled it out from under me so abruptly, so publicly. . . . I'll never feel the same about a job."[1]

Arnold had better results with his posthoneymoon work. *Predator* opened on June 12, 1987, and grossed almost $35 million in its first three weeks. *Predator* may be one of Arnold's most frightening movies. Arnold plays Dutch, a cigar-smoking Special Forces major. Dutch has a team of combat specialists whose primary function is to perform search-and-rescue missions behind enemy lines. Under false pretenses they are sent into the jungle by a former friend of Dutch's, CIA agent Dillon (played by Carl Weathers). Dillon accompanies them into the jungle where they are supposed to be rescuing a diplomat whose helicopter crashed in an area controlled by rebel guerrilla forces. The viewer soon realizes that the shot of some sort of spacecraft entering the earth's atmosphere at the very beginning of the movie is going to be somehow connected to Dutch's mission. No human enemy could have hung four

CIA agents upside down high in a tree and skinned them. Dutch and his team sense that they are up against more than just guerrillas. They soon accomplish their goal of finding and destroying a rebel encampment, although they are too late to rescue any of the rebels' captives. Dutch finds out that he has been duped by Dillon: Those captives had been an unsuccessful CIA team that had been sent in to destroy the rebel encampment. Mission accomplished, Dutch and his men head out into the jungle, where the real battle of the movie will be fought.

But there is something stalking them. One by one it picks off Dutch's men and Dillon. When the Predator gets Dillon, Arnold finally gets to use a modified version of the severed-arm gag he wanted to put into *Commando*. It is not funny, however, it is frightening. When the Predator hacks off Dillon's arm, the arm falls to the ground still clutching its machine gun. The unattached arm continues to jerk and fire off a few more rounds while Dillon screams in horror. By the time Dutch is the only remaining soldier, the audience begins to wonder how he will ever be able to defeat what they now know is an alien monster.

As usual, many of the critics missed the point. One went as far as to say, "It's arguably one of the emptiest, feeblest, most derivative scripts ever made as a major studio movie."[2] *Predator* is a classic confrontation between an incarnation of evil and a true warrior. The gruesomeness of the Predator's violence proves to the audience how evil he is. It is as if the Predator is searching for a worthy adversary and finally finds one in Dutch. In the final confrontation between Dutch and the Predator, the creature removes his armored helmet and high-tech weapons to fight Dutch in hand-to-hand combat. It seems as though Dutch doesn't stand a chance. Even the rippling muscles of Arnold Schwarzenegger are no match for the strength of this alien hunter of men. In the end it is Dutch's brains that defeat the creature. After all the violence and carnage of the movie the message is that the human mind is what we should ultimately value the most. Commenting on audience reaction, Arnold Schwarzenegger said,

> If some people are appalled by that [the violence in *Predator*] I understand that. It's just that if you have a picture like that and you don't see how vicious the enemy is or the monster or whatever it is then you don't have any tension. If the enemy is a nice guy you don't get the flavor of the movie and you don't sympathize with the heroes. They are sympathetic to me because I'm in danger . . . because I'm vulnerable.[3]

The filming of *Predator* was not without a hitch. At first Carl Weathers and Arnold had some problems getting along. Weathers supposedly was put off by the cigar smoke, but by the end of the movie, Weathers was smoking cigars along with many others. One other problem that concerned Arnold during the filming of *Predator* was the increasing danger of the stunts he was being asked to perform. There is great competition among the studios to make the biggest explosions and most dangerous-looking stunts, and the pressure was being felt by the directors, special-effects people, and the stunt men. The stunts Arnold had to perform were becoming increasingly dangerous. In one stunt, Arnold needed to swing from one tree to another on a vine. He accepted the fact that he would hit the landing tree hard, but he was not ready for what happened next. As he swung into the tree, an explosion was to go off above him to simulate a missed shot by the Predator. The explosion was much bigger than Arnold expected. As he clung to the tree he was soon being showered by falling leaves that had been set on fire by the explosion. Since Arnold was too high up in the tree to jump, all he could do was cling there and hope that he would not be burned severely.

The movie turned out to be another big hit for Arnold. Once again he was named Star of the Year by the National Association of Theatre Owners. Just prior to the release of *Predator,* on June 2, 1987, Arnold became the 1,847th star added to the Hollywood Walk of Fame.

Chapter Twelve

Running Man to Red Heat

From fighting the Predator in the jungles of Central America, Arnold went to fighting for his life on a game show in the future in *The Running Man*. As the film opens we see Arnold's character, Ben Richards, as a helicopter pilot for the federal police. He is on his way to Bakersfield, California, to put down a food riot, when he is ordered to fire into the crowd. Richards refuses to do this but is overpowered by his less sensitive crew. Richards's next stop is prison. When he escapes from prison and then is recaptured, he is offered a chance to participate in a game show. In this game show, guest criminals are given the chance literally to run for their lives. As they do so, professional "stalkers" hunt them down, while a studio audience screams for blood and wins door prizes. Richard Dawson, best known as the emcee of "The Family Feud" game show, plays Damon Killian, the ratings-hungry host of "The Running Man" show.

The government had called Richards the Butcher of Bakersfield when they edited the tapes of the night Richards refused to follow orders. The edited tapes made it seem as though Richards was personally responsible for the massacre of hundreds of innocent and hungry people. Once Richards starts playing the "game," one by one he defeats the killers who are the supposed heroes of the show. The underlying story line revolves around a group of rebels. They are trying to gain control of one of the government's satellite up-link stations so they can broadcast the truth to a brainwashed public.

It is the hope of the rebels that once they broadcast the truth, the public will rise up against the Fascist mind control of the government as put forth in shows like *The Running Man.* The show itself is an electronic version of the Colosseum of Rome, with the audience lusting for the blood of the gladiators. In this movie, Arnold ends up fighting the barbarians who are running the world in 2019. And as in all of Arnold's action movies, the good guys win despite seemingly overwhelming odds.

The Running Man was directed by Paul Michael Glaser with a script by Steven E. de Souza. When it was released in November 1987, it almost immediately became the top-grossing film in the country, taking in $10.5 million in the first week. As always Arnold took an active interest in the marketing of the movie and the audience response surveys. In the July 1988 *Cosmopolitan,* it was reported that *The Running Man* generated the most positive response by women in the audience of any of Arnold's movies to date. Arnold asked the producer how the women in the audience responded to the question, "What do you like about Arnold?" He was told that many of them responded by saying they "thought he had a cute a—."[1] Arnold responded, "I now know in which direction to take my next movie."

Although at the time Arnold may have been joking about the survey results, he seems to have taken them somewhat seriously. He starts his next movie wrapped only in a towel as he stalks drug dealers through a Russian gym and bathhouse. Arnold has remarked that he feels nudity just to help sell a movie is inappropriate. Nudity or near nudity is okay, however, if it helps to establish his character or is called for by the action of the scene. In *Red Heat* Arnold plays a Russian police officer who is sent to Chicago to pick up the Russian drug dealer who killed his partner in Moscow. *Red Heat* is an exciting movie from a number of viewpoints. Financially, it was the first movie that Arnold was paid $10 million for. Politically it was the first movie to benefit from the beginnings of glasnost in what was then called the Soviet Union. And it was the first time an American movie company had been allowed to shoot in Red Square.

Arnold had been in the Soviet Union about ten years prior to the filming of *Red Heat*, and was amazed at the differences. He saw that there were now a number of private businesses in Moscow, and the people were much more relaxed about many facets of their lives. Arnold had assumed that with the possible exception of a few bodybuilders, he would be unknown in the Soviet Union. The company was amazed when 5,000 people turned out to watch the filming in Red Square. Arnold was even more amazed to learn that videos of all his movies were hot properties on the black market. To his surprise, he had many fans in Moscow who had seen *Terminator*, *Commando*, and *Predator*.

This was the first time Arnold had a costar who is a major draw in his own right. Jim Belushi, who had starred in *Trading*

Arnold Schwarzenegger

Places and *Salvador,* plays Chicago police officer Art Ridzik. Belushi's character is assigned to escort Ivan Danko, Arnold's character, around Chicago. Together they pursue Viktor, the Russian drug dealer who has escaped from the police.

Although Belushi and Arnold play it mostly straight, there is an underlying current of humor. There is also the notion that, despite their differences, Danko and Ridzik feel the same way about getting the bad guys. In fact, according to Roger Ebert, "*Red Heat* works because Schwarzenegger and Belushi are both basically comic actors."[2] One way that *Red Heat* differs from the usual portrayal of Soviets in American movies is that Danko is neither a bad guy nor does he wish to defect to the West. At the end of the movie, after he and Belushi have triumphed, he proudly returns to Moscow to continue fighting for right in his own country. It forces the viewer to think about the fact that patriotism is not something to which Americans have exclusive rights.

Walter Hill, the writer-director of *Red Heat,* felt that Arnold's face—the face of a warrior—was the key to his success. In *Red Heat* Hill let Belushi do most of the talking and showed in Arnold's face Danko's reactions to what was going on around him. "Arnold's like a modern Theseus," said Hill. "He has almost a mythic relationship with his audience. He loves being their hero."[3]

Belushi was impressed with Arnold. Off camera, he began calling Arnold the Professor since their on-screen roles were reversed and Arnold did all the talking.

Red Heat was Schwarzenegger's ninth movie since the 1982 release of *Conan the Barbarian.* Although Arnold kept up a blistering pace of moviemaking, he remained active in other areas as well. His real estate and other investments continued to thrive, as did his marriage to Maria. Arnold told *McCall's* magazine, June 1992, that the "marriage is much more of an equal partnership than outsiders might imagine. . . . She reads my scripts, and her opinion weighs heavily on all my decisions."[4]

When they were both at home in Pacific Palisades, their life, as Maria put it, was "a nice life, boringly normal, like anybody else's."[5] Arnold and Maria enjoy dining with friends at home, although Arnold kids Maria "about her woeful cooking skills, telling her she needs a road map to find the kitchen."[6] Maria retaliates by teasing Arnold about his conservative politics. They also enjoy playing tennis together and riding their horses. At the time Arnold had an Andalusian horse and rode Western while Maria had a hunter-jumper and rode English. They also have two Labrador retrievers named Conan and Strudel. They enjoy skiing and join Maria's family in Aspen, Colorado, for Christmas and skiing.

After losing her job on CBS "Morning News," Maria went to work for NBC as the cohost, with Boyd Matson, of "Sunday Today." She also did a monthly news program for young people called "Main Street." Her duties later expanded to include anchoring the weekend edition of the NBC "Nightly News."

During this time, Arnold remained active with the Special Olympics. When the Special Olympics were started in 1968, organizers' only expectations were that those participating would enjoy the event. As time has gone on, the expectations have changed and those participating have become trained athletes who happen to have mental or physical handicaps. Arnold maintains his position as the Special Olympics national weight-training coach. In 1987 Arnold held a press conference with two Special Olympians, Mark and Mike Hembd, twins who both have Down's syndrome. Mark and Mike had been weight training to improve their performance as swimmers and did a weight-lifting exhibition at the press conference. In a *Los Angeles Times* story, their mother, Sandra Hembd, paid Arnold an immense compliment when she was quoted as saying that her sons "live in a black-and-white world. They don't know if Arnold Schwarzenegger is a governor or a movie star. But they picked up on the fact that he was real sincere."[7]

Chapter Thirteen

Arnold and His Twin

By the time *Red Heat* was released, Arnold had built a fortress in the movie industry and people were definitely coming to him to do action-adventure movies. Arnold however, wanted to come out of the fortress and do a comedy. When he asked the studios to send him scripts for comedies, they put him off. They told him that there weren't any that would be suitable. Finally, in the mid-1980s, Arnold met with Ivan Reitman, who had directed such comedies as *Meatballs*, *Stripes*, *Ghostbusters*, and *Ghostbusters II*. Arnold and Reitman discussed Arnold's desire to do a comedy.

As a result of that meeting, Reitman hired writers to come up with a concept for a movie that eventually evolved into the script for *Twins*. The final script for *Twins* was written by William Davies, William Osborne, Timothy Harris, and Herschel Weingrod. The story line is that a genetics lab combines the genes from six ideal men and selects a "superwoman" to be the mother. The intent is to produce the perfect human specimen. Arnold's character, Julius Benedict, is the successful offspring of the experiment. However, there was one problem with the experiment. The mother had twins. Julius, however, does not learn about his fraternal twin brother until his thirty-fifth birthday. When he learns that he has a brother, he decides to leave the institute, where he has been kept isolated from the everyday world, and search for his twin.

Julius's twin brother, Vincent, played by Danny DeVito, who is to comedy movies what Arnold is to action-adventure movies, turns out to be his total opposite. Just the idea of six-foot-two-inch, 210-pound Arnold Schwarzenegger and the diminutive DeVito as fraternal twins is funny enough to attract an audience. What no one in Hollywood had realized before *Twins* is that Arnold is the perfect straight man to pit against the wise-cracking and mischievous DeVito.

Once Julius finds Vincent, he convinces him that together they should search for their mother. Their search is full of misadventure involving a pair of sisters and a stolen jet-fuel-injection system. As in many comedies, the plot is secondary to the chemistry of the characters. In *Twins*, Arnold and DeVito find the chemistry that all great comedy teams have and make it come alive on the screen. The movie premiered on December 5, 1988, at the Kennedy Center in Washington, D.C. For once, many reviewers were in agreement with the audience's reaction and wrote generally positive reviews of *Twins*.

Reitman was quoted in an article written by Jack Mathews that Arnold "worked as any other actor (does). He took the role seriously, he rehearsed, he asked questions. . . . It was very easy to make comedy come out of his character."[1] Arnold attributed his success in part to the fact that the audience does not expect comedy from a big tough guy and therefore it works better than if a little guy had done the same gag or delivered the same line.[2]

This was another movie where Arnold could laugh all the way to the bank. Both Arnold and DeVito had forgone any up-front salary guarantee in exchange for healthy percentages of the profits. In the first two weekends, *Twins* grossed $22.2 million and by mid–1991 the movie had made over $120 million. Reportedly, Arnold's share of the movie's profit is around $30 million. In an interview with Barry Koltnow, Arnold mentions that "since *Twins*, about 70 percent of the scripts sent to me by the studios are comedies."[3] Arnold thought that it was pretty funny since before *Twins* he was told there weren't any comedies that were suitable for him.

Maria was also making progress with her career. In 1989 she signed a four-year contract with NBC News that was reported to include a salary of $475,000 a year. Despite her new contract, Maria was beginning to tire of the grueling schedule of being near the top of the network news, which is produced in New York, while she lived on the West Coast. In the October 1988 interview in *McCall's* Maria talked about one week where she needed to fly from Los Angeles to Israel, back to Los Angeles, then to Jordan, then to New York, back to Jordan, and then finally back to Los Angeles. As time went on, she wanted to spend more time at home.

When she became pregnant in 1989 she planned to take a three-month maternity leave after the baby was born, and then return to her same job. On December 13, 1989, Maria gave birth to Katherine Eunice Schwarzenegger. Prior to Katherine's birth, Arnold was reportedly calling her "the Schwarzen-shriver."

Neither Arnold nor Maria could have predicted the impact that Katherine would have on their lives. Prior to her birth they had been two very successful people who loved each other. They spent as much time together as their busy schedules allowed. The birth of Katherine made them a family. Both Arnold and Maria felt the family bond strongly. They changed their schedules so they could spend more time together as a threesome. Arnold told *Redbook* that he "never realized how much joy being a new father can bring. It's a lot of fun. I even sometimes change diapers."[4] Maria kept extending her maternity leave until she was summoned to New York to meet with network executives. They wanted her back at work and Maria wanted to anchor the weekend shows from the West Coast. The executives refused. Maria was quoted in *McCall's* (June 1992) as having told the network executives that "you shouldn't have to choose between a job and a family." Maria's iron will won out over the men at the top of NBC. She now does a series of specials originating on the West Coast under the title "First Person with Maria Shriver."

Arnold and Maria spent much of the first year of Katherine's life following her around with a video camera documenting all the important firsts: first tooth, first steps, first word, and so on. Arnold told Barry Koltnow of the *San Francisco Examiner* that the birth of Katherine also had an impact on his thinking about movies. He wanted to stay loyal to his action-adventure audience but he found himself thinking about making movies that a parent could let a child of six or eight watch. Arnold also said he had made changes in his daily routine so that he could spend more time with his new daughter. He went as far as to say, "I try to schedule my life around my child." Arnold and Maria,

Arnold and His Twin

although brought up in different worlds, both come from families that have strong traditional family values. They hope to pass that to their own children. Arnold, however, told *Redbook* that he was "not going to make an effort to create the same sort of atmosphere and upbringing and childhood that [he] had." Arnold went on to say that "it wouldn't be natural." Obviously there would many differences in the lifestyle of this family of Schwarzeneggers. Arnold made it clear that he hasn't set any domestic rules for raising his children.

Arnold has received almost no personally negative press. He had been criticized as an actor by reviewers but his personal life appeared above reproach. In 1990 an English journalist tried to change that. Wendy Leigh wrote and Congdon and Weed published *Arnold, An Unauthorized Biography*. Leigh's attempted character assassination of Hollywood's biggest star was a flop, selling only 30,000 copies. Arnold had worked hard to build himself a positive public image. He worked just as hard to minimize any negative publicity from the book. Leigh's portrayal of Arnold Schwarzenegger suggests that Arnold was a young man who was driven to succeed first in bodybuilding and then in Hollywood. Her condemnation of him often depends on seeing the sacrifices he made to achieve his success as negative. Her attempt to paint Arnold as some sort of monster lacks substance and is clouded by a strong use of pop psychology. Harry Plotnick, Leigh's publisher, told the *Los Angeles Times* that he attributed the lack of success of the book in part to the fact that "people weren't as interested in a negative picture of Schwarzenegger as we thought they would be."[5] Arnold reacted to the book publicly by telling *Time* magazine, "I don't want to give a third-grade journalist any credibility."[6]

In March 1989 Arnold hosted the Arnold Schwarzenegger Classic bodybuilding tournament in Columbus, Ohio. It was the richest bodybuilding tournament to date with $125,000 in prize money. Arnold felt that bodybuilders should receive the sort of attention that other major sports figures receive. In March 1990, Arnold created another first in bodybuilding. The 1990 Arnold Schwarzenegger Classic was the first professional bodybuilding tournament that required a drug test for the participants. Drug testing had already been implemented on the amateur level.

Nineteen-ninety brought another first for Arnold. He moved from in front of the cameras as an actor to behind the camera as a director. Joel Silver, the producer of *Commando* and *Predator*, knew that Arnold was interested in directing. When Silver became the executive producer of HBO's "Tales from the Crypt," a horror series, he offered Arnold the opportunity to direct a half-hour segment. Silver sent Arnold twenty possible scripts and Arnold selected one called "The Switch." In it, an old, very wealthy man named Webster falls in love with a beautiful young woman. However, the woman is unwilling to accept him physically. First Webster spends $1 million to trade faces surgically with a handsome young man. When this fails to win the girl, Webster spends another $2 million to get the younger man's muscular upper body. This almost works until the girl sees his spindly old-looking legs. Webster then gives up the remaining $3 million of his fortune to get the younger man's legs. In the ironic ending, the girl runs away with the younger man who now has the old man's face and body but also has his $6 million. Arnold felt that directing would be an exciting challenge for him. He had stated a number of times that he likes to be in control of things, and directing would give him total control over the project. It was also a little frightening because Arnold always wants to succeed no matter what he's doing, and directing was something new that he was unsure about.

Arnold and His Twin

What the critics never understood was how much I respond to challenges. That's what directing is about. That's what acting was all about after bodybuilding. Maybe there's something else out there I haven't thought of yet.[7]

It may have been a challenge, but Arnold's directing debut was a success. He earned the respect of the actors on the project and enjoyed the intellectual and artistic creativity demanded by directing. Arnold's next directing effort was a made-for-TV movie that aired on TNT on April 13, 1992, entitled *Christmas in Connecticut*. It is a remake of a 1945 movie that had starred Barbara Stanwyck. Arnold's version starred Kris Kristofferson and Dyan Cannon. Arnold plans eventually to do a full-length motion picture.

Chapter Fourteen

Conan Versus the Couch Potatoes

As early as 1984 Arnold had shown his political colors by attending the Republican National Convention in Dallas and by financially supporting Republicans in California. Arnold found that the more conservative, business-oriented Republicans fit his personal philosophy better than the more liberal Democrats. At the 1988 Republican Convention, Arnold was part of one of the "caucus teams." These teams were made up of members of the Reagan administration and Bush loyalists who made the rounds of the state delegations. In the fall of 1988 he campaigned for Vice President George Bush as he ran for the presidency. Arnold traveled throughout the Midwest with Bush as he campaigned. During one flight on Air Force Two, the *Los Angeles Times* reported that Bush was discussing the sad state of physical fitness in the United States. Arnold spoke up and said, "If I can be of any help, let me know."[1] From this conversation, an idea grew.

Arnold is often teased about his politics by his wife and her family. Maria jokingly told *McCall's*,[2] "when you marry someone, you marry them for sickness and health. [Republican politics] are Arnold's sickness." Joking aside, Arnold admires the dedication and sense of service that the Kennedy family embodies. He had already become an active participant in the Special Olympics but his political support of George Bush gave him the opportunity to do more. After Bush was elected, Arnold was appointed chairman of the President's Council on Physical Fitness and Sports.

Things looked good for Arnold as he met with President-elect Bush's transition team after the fall 1988 election and discussed the possible appointment. According to the *Saturday Evening Post*, he told the team that he wanted to restore the Council to the prominence it had during the presidency of John Kennedy. The Washington rumor mill had it that "Conan the Republican," as President Bush called him, would get the job.

President Bush also showed that he understood the problems of a prominent Republican being married to a member of the most famous Democratic family in the country. President-elect and Mrs. Bush attended the December 1988 premiere of *Twins*, which was held at the Kennedy Center in Washington, D.C. In speaking to the press about the movie and his friendship with the larger of its two stars, Bush was quoted in the *Saturday Evening Post* as saying, "There are all kinds of courage. There is the courage of my friend Arnold Schwarzenegger, who more than once campaigned with me across the country . . . and then returned home each time to take the heat from his in-laws."[3]

On January 22, 1990, it became official: Arnold Schwarzenegger was appointed the chairman of the President's Council on Physical Fitness and Sports. The position is strictly voluntary and the budget of the council comes primarily from donations and corporate sponsorships. Over the objections of those around him, Arnold vowed to visit all fifty states to meet with governors, legislators, students, and other key people. The concern was that if he promised to visit all fifty states, he would be obligated to deliver. What those who objected didn't understand was that Arnold doesn't do things halfway. Once he realized that educational issues were directed at the state and local level, he knew it was important to take his message to the states. He had wanted the appointment as chairman of the council because he felt that there is a real need to get the kids of America, and their parents and grandparents as well, off the couches and onto the playing fields. Arnold totally agrees with the president's council motto: "It's just as important to grow up fit as it is to grow up smart." And Arnold felt we need to start by making physical education classes a part of every school day for every school-age child in the United States.

Arnold undertook his fitness crusade with the same determination he does everything. "I owe America," Arnold said after his appointment. "Here's my chance to give something back."[4] It was at this time that Arnold acquired a Gulfstream II private jet, hired a pilot and a flight attendant, and set out to visit all fifty states. Arnold understands one important thing about American society: the power of the press. Throughout his career as a bodybuilder and especially as an author and actor, Arnold has demonstrated an amazing knack for getting the attention of the media. And once Arnold gets the media's attention he makes sure they hear the message that he wants to give. As Arnold began his tour, it was obvious that this would be his most ambitious attempt at using the media.

Conan Versus the Couch Potatoes

Arnold felt that if enough people heard his message enough times, then people would begin to do something about it. The message is straightforward. America needs to wake up and take an active interest in the physical fitness of everyone in the country. Arnold told Peter Carlson of the *Washington Post* that "physical fitness can be sold to American kids just like Ninja Turtle cereal and $100 inflatable sneakers."[5]

A typical visit to a state involved a meeting with the governor and other state-elected officials, press conferences, and meetings with parent and teacher groups. Probably the most important stops in each state were the school visits. Arnold would get a group of students exercising while the cameras rolled and he spoke of the importance of physical fitness. Arnold also served as the president's representative to a number of sports and fitness-related events. He was the keynote speaker at the three-day Northwest Youth Fitness Conference in Washington. He represented President Bush at the 1990 Goodwill Games held in Seattle, Washington, and at the 1991 International Special Olympics. He also headed the American delegation to the 1992 Summer Olympics in Barcelona, Spain.

Arnold's fitness crusade was not just media hype and personal appearances. He also has specific proposals that he made to the states along with suggestions about how and why they should be implemented. In typical Republican fashion, Arnold didn't feel that the federal government should pay for an expanded fitness program. Arnold suggested that the health insurance companies should consider getting involved. If people become more physically fit they will need less in the way of medical care, thus costing health insurance companies less. And he backs up his claims with statistics.

In an article that Arnold wrote for *The New York Times*, he said, "40 percent of children ages five to eight already exhibit at least one heart-disease risk factor—that is, obesity, elevated cholesterol, high blood pressure or physical inactivity."[6] He went on to say that the United States spent $230 billion on health care in 1980, and by 1990 that had almost tripled to $606 billion. Arnold stated that it could triple again in the next ten years if unfit children become unfit and unhealthy adults.

Arnold used an example from his movie *Kindergarten Cop*, in which he worked with a group of aspiring five-year-old actresses and actors. There were a few scenes in the movie where Arnold had his students exercising. He claims that the more they exercised the more fun the kids had. He states that it is extremely important to begin exercising at an early age. Patterns established as children will hopefully continue throughout their lives. Arnold was also amazed to learn that of fifty states only one—Illinois—has a law on the books that requires daily physical education for students in kindergarten through twelfth grade.

To stress the importance of physical fitness, May has been designated as National Physical Fitness and Sports Month. On May 1, 1990, Arnold and President Bush began hosting the annual Great American Workout on the south lawn of the White House to kick off the month's activities. In 1992 the activities at the White House were held in conjunction with similar events in many state capitals. For 1992 the special theme for the Great American Workout was family fitness. Arnold has also made fitness for older Americans a priority.

Arnold told readers in his article for *The New York Times* that "parents must "make fitness a family affair. So many parents say they don't have the time. Nonsense. If they can spend a couple of hours watching television at night, they surely can spend 30 minutes going for a brisk walk, playing ball or engaging in some other vigorous activity with their youngsters.'' To prove to the public that he was serious about getting America fit, Arnold gave up smoking his Cuban Davidoff cigars. At least he doesn't smoke in public anymore.

It is hard to gauge how much of a change Arnold has made in America's attitudes toward fitness. If the amount of coverage he has received as chairman of the President's Council on Physical Fitness and Sports is any indication, then his impact is surely substantial. Arnold has gotten more media attention as chairman of the council than for any of his books or movies. His endeavors as the chairman of the council have been reported in all the major magazines and newspapers, as well as in magazines like *National Geographic World* and *Tomorrow's Business Leader*. Whenever Arnold visits a state, he is covered by all the local media. He is bound to be seen on the local TV news shaking hands with the governor on the steps of the capitol and in the schools encouraging children to exercise.

In April 1992, Arnold once again did what the skeptics had said was impossible. Arnold visited Ohio, his fiftieth state. While at the Bluffsview Elementary School in Worthington, he received a congratulatory phone call from President Bush, who was on Air Force One. Now, that's the way to make an impression.

Arnold has been so energetic and forceful with his fitness crusade that it has led many cynics to speculate that perhaps Arnold has a new master plan that includes running for office. Ronald Reagan led the way from acting to politics and many think Arnold will follow. Arnold has continued to deny any rumors that he is considering running for public office.

Chapter Fifteen

∎

Martian Spy to Kindergarten Cop

▩ ▩ ▩ ▩ ▩ ▩

In 1989 Arnold Schwarzenegger began filming *Total Recall*. The movie idea and script, in one form or another, had been around Hollywood for over ten years. It had been owned by a number of different studios, but, because of the cost, no one had attempted to begin filming. Arnold had almost made the movie when Dino De Laurentiis owned the rights to it. But De Laurentiis and Arnold could not come to terms. When De Laurentiis's film company folded, Arnold convinced the people at Carolco to buy the script.

This was to be Arnold's deal. He had script and director approval as well as a $10 million salary. Arnold also helped raise the $60 million it would take to make this science fiction thriller. At the time it was the most expensive movie ever made. One way in which money was raised for the movie was through commercial endorsements. There are twenty-eight different brand names shown in the movie. Because of this, the movie was criticized by the Center for the Study of Commercialism, headed by consumer activist Ralph Nader.

To direct the movie Arnold selected the Dutch filmmaker Paul Verhoeven. Arnold liked the job Verhoeven had done with the hit movie *Robocop*, and *Total Recall* was to be a similar type of movie. Some critics have dubbed this genre "new bad future" as they show our society in a future state of social decay. *Mad Max, Terminator, RoboCop, Aliens,* and others fit into this genre.

Vic Armstrong, who had been Harrison Ford's double in the *Indiana Jones* movies, was selected to coordinate the stunts. Jefferson Dawn got the job of creating all the blood and gore. Dawn also supervised the elaborate makeup that was needed to create the humans who have become mutants because of exposure to the harsh environment of Mars. The mutants play an important part in the story as they are trying to rebel against the colony's evil administrator, Cohaagen.

Total Recall is probably the most complex of all of the films Arnold has made. For the segment of the audience that goes to see blood, gore, and explosions, the movie has all that, but there is more. Arnold's character, Doug Quaid, is not who he appears to be—not even to himself. Quaid appears to be a construction worker on Earth in the twenty-first century. But in reality he is a former henchman for the totalitarian Cohaagen who has had his memory erased and replaced with the memories of Doug Quaid. Quaid is haunted by dreams of Mars, where he thinks he has never been. In an attempt to quiet his dreams and satisfy his curiosity about Mars, Quaid signs up for a vacation memory implant at a company called Rekall, Inc.

When they attempt to implant the vacation trip to Mars, the doctors at Rekall discover that Quaid has had a memory erasure that causes their programmed memories to go haywire.

Although Quaid cannot remember his erased identity, the fact that he is aware that he had one is enough to bring out the agents of Cohaagen. As they try to capture Quaid, the action begins and all the subtleties of the plot are unfolded. Quaid receives a suitcase that is a legacy from his former self. From a computer-generated message he learns about the rebellion on Mars. He also realizes that he has some secret knowledge about the previous inhabitants of the planet and the giant reactor they have left behind—a secret that will unlock the stranglehold of Cohaagen and free the people of the planet. Quaid decides that he must seek the answers to the mysteries surrounding him and heads for Mars.

On Mars, Quaid makes his way to Venusville, the home turf of the mutants and headquarters for the rebellion against Cohaagen. The rebels are convinced that as Quaid, Arnold's character is on their side and take him to their leader, Kuato. Like many mutants Kuato is psychic and is able to extract the secret deep within Quaid's lost memory. In the most ironic twist of the movie it turns out that Quaid has plotted his own double cross to capture Kuato. The rebel leader is killed and Quaid is brought before Cohaagen to learn of his part in the crushing of the rebels. There is one last twist to this thriller. The Quaid that has been implanted in the memories of this evil double agent believes in goodness and the rebel cause, and ultimately wins.

Filming *Total Recall* was a real challenge for the film crew. All the scenes were shot on sets made for the movie. It took over 500 painters and carpenters to make the sixty sets, at a cost of $5 million. The movie was filmed in Mexico City, Mexico, at Churubusco Studios and took twenty weeks to shoot.

Martian Spy to Kindergarten Cop

While in Mexico, Arnold had a portable gym set up in one of the offices of the studio so he could continue his daily workouts. He also had an office in the motor home that served as his dressing room on the set. From this office he stayed in touch with the media. Arnold also took it upon himself to keep everyone on the set loose. Rachel Ticotin, who plays his rebel girlfriend on Mars, Melina, told *Los Angeles Times* writer Jack Mathews that Arnold "teases everybody and the more vulnerable they get, the more he goes for it." She continued, saying that Arnold "has so much warmth, nobody really takes it personally. No matter what he says . . . it's okay."[1] In the same article, coproducer Ronald Shusett told of being awoken from a nap by a bucket of ice water being poured on his lap by Arnold. Shusett said that "Arnold's locker-room humor has kept nerves from getting frayed on a grueling 20-week location shoot."

In its original version, *Total Recall* received an X rating and was sent back for additional editing to tone down the four most violent scenes. *Total Recall* premiered on May 31, 1990, at the Hollywood Pacific Theatre in Los Angeles and then opened nationwide on June first. It was an overnight smash hit. In its first three days, *Total Recall* earned $26.4 million to make it the picture with the year's biggest three-day opening. The movie earned over $100 million in its first forty days to make it the number one movie of the summer of 1990. During this whole time Arnold stayed on top of the publicity for the movie. Reportedly he was told that *Total Recall* would make it onto the covers of twelve national magazines. Arnold is said to have replied, "What, only twelve? I thought I had fifteen!"

Arnold told Ryan Murphy in the *Miami Herald* after *Total Recall* was out that "I have this plan. What I will do in the future is every second film will be a comedy with the first film being an action-adventure movie."[2] What he did instead was to make a movie that was a combination comedy-action-adventure film. As the *Kindergarten Cop*, Arnold tried to satisfy both his audiences at once.

In *Kindergarten Cop*, Arnold plays John Kimble, a Los Angeles police detective who has been trying to bust a big-time drug dealer. The dealer is behind bars temporarily and Kimble needs the dealer's ex-wife to testify against him. Kimble gets a tip that the woman and her kindergarten-age son are living in Astoria, Oregon. He doesn't know what she looks like or under what name she is living. So Kimble goes undercover as a kindergarten teacher in an attempt to discover the identity of the woman and her son.

There is an old saying in the acting world that you should never work with animals or children as they steal the scene every time. Arnold read the script for *Kindergarten Cop* and wanted to make the movie. He realized, however, that it would not be an easy task. He felt there was only one person who could successfully direct him in the film and that was *Twins* director, Ivan Reitman. The studio was reluctant. Reitman was working on another film and they wanted to get going. Arnold stood firm and eventually convinced both the studio and Reitman that he was the man for the job. The fact that the studio was paying Arnold $12 million, the most money ever paid an actor for a nonsequel, perhaps had something to do with them letting Arnold get his way.

Once Reitman had signed on to direct, he was faced with the problem of finding the right kids to be part of Arnold's kindergarten class in the movie. Reitman rented a school in Los Angeles and auditioned 2,000 children. Most of them were nonactors, between the ages of four and seven. He needed to find the thirty students who would be in Kimble's class in the movie. When they had narrowed it down to about 250 kids, Arnold joined in the audition process.

The kids were fascinated with Arnold's muscles. They asked him so many questions he said he felt as if he had been to see a psychiatrist by the time he was finished. "They wanted to climb me," he said. "All day long, they would grab my legs, hang onto my arms. . . . I was like a jungle gym to them."[3]

Although Arnold was worried about how he was going to relate to the children in the movie, he came up with an interesting solution. "It dawned on me that physical fitness would be a way to approach them. I asked them to do jumping jacks and 100 kids enthusiastically started to do jumping jacks. We started exercising and from that point on I had them totally on my side."[4] In talking about Arnold's working with the children in the movie, Reitman was quoted in the same article as saying, "I think they softened his heart. He really got into the film."

Reitman and Arnold had to do things a little differently when it came to filming the movie. Normally a director will call for a number of takes of a particular scene until he is satisfied that everyone has done it just the way he wants it. Working with young children, they soon learned that after the first take the kids would start to lose interest. By going with only one take, Reitman was able to overcome the short attention span of the children and create a movie that was really funny and still believable.

Arnold's portrayal of the tough cop almost losing the battle of the classroom was well done. The part where many critics felt Reitman went a little too far was in the final confrontation between Kimble and the drug dealer-father who has also come to Astoria for his son. The violence at the end of the movie earned the movie a PG–13 rating. It showed the hard side of John Kimble and the contrast was probably a valid one to

Arnold Schwarzenegger

make. The PG–13 rating, however, caused many parents to keep their children from seeing a movie that they would have otherwise enjoyed.

Even without the younger children who would have seen the movie had it had a PG rating, *Kindergarten Cop* was yet another box office smash for Arnold Schwarzenegger. *Kindergarten Cop* earned $11.3 million in the first five days, $44.8 million in the first two weeks, and ended up earning over $120 million. Many movie critics also liked it: "Wow, Arnold Schwarzenegger has been in some tough spots in his movies but you haven't seen him really sweat until you've seen him alone in a room with 30 five-year-olds!"[5] "Ah-nold . . . really is funny. . . . What makes [this movie] such frisky fun is Schwarzenegger's obvious delight in acting silly. He has an easy rapport with the tykes."[6]

If *Kindergarten Cop* was the comedy, then according to Arnold, an action-adventure movie should follow. It was time for the haunting words of the Terminator to come true. When the cyborg terminator said "I'll be back," everyone who is an Arnold Schwarzenegger fan hoped that meant there would be a sequel. They were not to be disappointed.

Chapter Sixteen

Hasta la Vista, Baby!

Arnold had learned from his Conan movies that it didn't pay to change directors. When it came time to do the sequel to *The Terminator* the same basic crew was brought together. One of the biggest challenges of *Terminator 2: Judgment Day* was coming up with a workable idea for the script. At one point James Cameron thought about having Arnold play both the good and the bad terminators. They eventually decided to create a new, sleeker terminator, the T–1000 played by Robert Patrick. Cameron had envisioned the original terminator as an infiltration unit and had changed the part to fit Arnold. The T–1000 is the perfect infiltration unit, able to change itself into any human form.

Those who had seen the original terminator and its relentless drive to destroy its target, and heard the famous line "I'll be back," probably expected Arnold to take up the pursuit where he had left off. In a clever twist, Arnold's Terminator has been reprogrammed to go back and protect the young John Connor from the T–1000 that is out to kill him. Cameron, with his two terminators, is able to show his audience that technology itself is neither good nor bad. It is what is done with the technology that matters. The reprogrammed Terminator, played by Arnold, is as intent on saving John Connor and doing what the boy tells him as the original terminator had been in killing Sarah Connor in the first movie.

> We've tried for so long to make this movie [*Terminator 2*]. I'm talking about from the time we finished shooting the first one. Jim [Cameron] and I always felt that this was a good story that could lend itself to a sequel.
>
> But one has to be very careful with sequels. As you know, some people do them just because there's a potential moneymaker there. But that shouldn't be your only motivation. The main motivation should be, is it really a story that could have ongoing chapters that people will be interested in?[1]

Although some critics were disappointed in the story line of *Terminator 2*, almost all were impressed by the special effects of the movie, as well they should have been. The special effects used in *T2* cost over $17 million and were so revolutionary that they may have changed the way movies are made. There were a total of 800 stunt-man days used in filming *T2*, and Arnold told Arsenio Hall that the catering costs for *T2* were more than the total $6.9 million spent to make the original, *Terminator*. The grand total for the most expensive movie ever made was almost $100 million.

Industrial Light and Magic (ILM), the company created by

Hasta la Vista, Baby!

George Lucas to do the special effects for the *Star Wars* movies, was hired to do the special effects for *T2*. The major technique used by ILM to create the special effects of the T–1000 is *digitizing,* also called digital compositing. The picture image from the film is transferred into a computer. One frame of film, which lasts $\frac{1}{24}$ of a second on the screen, requires twenty megabytes of computer memory. The average school textbook would probably take less memory. The text for this book took up less than one-half of one megabyte. ILM's computers have memories measured in gigabytes. A gigabyte is one billion bytes of memory.

Once the images are entered into the computer, a graphic artist can change the image in unlimited ways. The image can be added to other entered images or to images created solely by the computer. In *T2* there are approximately forty computer-altered scenes. One of the most amazing is the scene where the T–1000 is able to walk through a steel grate. Reportedly, ILM invested $3.5 million in additional computer hardware to do the work on *T2*. Some have predicted that the technology being developed by ILM and others will ultimately eliminate the need for stuntpeople. It may also make obsolete the so-called "creature shops" that make monsters and other creatures for the movies. With this technology actors who are long dead can be brought back to star with living actors. Coca-Cola went on to do just that in their television commercials that use the likes of Gene Kelly, Humphrey Bogart, Groucho Marx, and others alongside the pop singer/dancer Paula Abdul.

Along more conventional special-effect lines, a full working model of Arnold was built for the film along with a working model of Arnold from the waist up. A working Terminator head was also used. Throughout the movie there are an elaborate series of crashes and chases, enough to satisfy even the hungriest action junkie. Even the actors redesigned themselves to better fit into the movie. Robert Patrick studied insects and the way they move to make his character seem less human. And Linda Hamilton, who recreated her role as Sarah Connor, trimmed down and muscled up for her part. She studied the martial arts and learned to use various weaponry, all to be convincing as a mother-turned-warrior in a battle to save her son and humanity.

The big budget did not stop once the movie was finished. The party held at the Century Plaza Hotel in Los Angeles for the opening cost Carolco and the distributor Tri-Star $450,000. The advertising budget for the movie was reported to be $25 million worldwide. After spending all this money, there must have been some very worried people when the movie opened on July 2, 1991. But there was no need to worry. By the end of October 1991, the *Los Angeles Times* reported that *Terminator 2: Judgment Day* had earned almost $200 million. The movie set records around the world.

Since *Terminator 2*, Arnold Schwarzenegger has become the biggest star who has ever blasted his way across movie screens. It has been reported that his latest film paid him his biggest salary ever: around $25 million.[2] No doubt he earned it; he has never failed to deliver a profit at the box office.

Outside the movie world Arnold remains busy handling his investments in restaurants and real estate. The first restaurant he invested in is Planet Hollywood, located at 140 West Fifty-seventh Street in New York City. The restaurant has other celebrity investors: Sylvester Stallone, Bruce Willis, and others joined Arnold in putting up the $15 million that was needed to open Planet Hollywood. The restaurant serves a California-style menu and is decorated with actual props from well-known movies. R2D2 and C3P0 from *Star Wars* are there, as is James

Hasta la Vista, Baby!

Dean's motorcycle from *Rebel Without a Cause* and, of course, a Terminator model. As people eat their meals, clips from movies are shown continuously on the six movie screens around the room.

The president of Planet Hollywood is Robert Earl, who, with Keith Barish, is a part of the Hard Rock Café success. Earl expects to open Planet Hollywoods throughout the world—eight more are in the planning stages. The New York Hard Rock Café serves about 750,000 guests a year and has sales of over $20 million. Planet Hollywood should be another success for Arnold and the other investors if it can do anything near what the Hard Rock Cafés have done.

On the home front things are busy as well. Arnold and Maria still live in Pacific Palisades, California, in the same house that Arnold bought before they got married. Their second daughter, Christina Aurelia Schwarzenegger, was born on July 23, 1991, and they are expecting a third child in October 1993.

The experience of Planet Hollywood has encouraged Arnold to get involved in a restaurant in Santa Monica. With the help of Robert Earl and others from Planet Hollywood, Arnold has opened Schatzi on Main. Schatzi is the German word for sweetheart and is what Arnold calls his daughters. Schatzi is a casual restaurant where the waiters wear Hawaiian shirts and the menu is simple but varied.

As if restaurants, real estate, and movies weren't enough, Arnold has just accepted another business responsibility. Joe Gold recently stepped down as chairman of World Gym and World Gym Licensing and named Arnold Schwarzenegger as his successor. Arnold and many other professional bodybuilders had trained in Joe's original gym in Santa Monica and were in part responsible for the success of his 150-gym chain. Arnold quoted the seventy-year-old Gold in a *Los Angeles Times* article as saying, "I want to make sure [World Gyms] goes into the right hands before anything happens to me."[3] And in his mind there were no better hands to guide the future of the gym than those of Arnold Schwarzenegger.

Arnold has finally succumbed to the Hollywood penchant for exotic cars. He was the first private citizen to own a Hummer, a street-legal version of the military's new all-wheel drive vehicle, the same vehicle that transported many of the Desert Storm soldiers across the deserts of Saudi Arabia, Kuwait, and Iraq. It seems fitting that the hero of so many action-adventure movies would have a military-style vehicle rather than a small sports car.

It may be a long time before anyone comes close to being as big a box-office star as Arnold Schwarzenegger. As this book went to press, a movie that sounds like it is named for him, *The Last Action Hero,* was released in June 1993. It stars Arnold in the title role and costars eleven-year-old Austin O'Brien, who falls into a movie he is watching and ends up sharing the hero's adventure.

Arnold has also been busy on the fitness front with a book, *Arnold's Fitness for Kids,* and a video, *The Fitness Express,* which can be rented for free at 25,000 video outlets around the country. Like the characters he plays, Arnold has become a true American Hero.

Appendix One
Bodybuilding Titles

1965 .... Junior Mr. Europe (Germany)
1966 .... Best Built Man of Europe (Germany)
1966 .... Mr. Europe (Germany)
1966 .... International Powerlifting Championship (Germany)
1967 .... NABBA Mr. Universe, Amateur (Great Britain)
1968 .... NABBA Mr. Universe, Professional (Great Britain)
1968 .... German Powerlifting Championship
1968 .... IFBB Mr. International (Mexico)
1969 .... IFBB Mr. Universe, Amateur (U.S.A.)
1969 .... NABBA Mr. Universe, Professional (Great Britain)
1970 .... NABBA Mr. Universe, Professional (Great Britain)
1970 .... Mr. World (U.S.A.)
1970 .... IFBB Mr. Olympia (U.S.A.)
1971 .... IFBB Mr. Olympia (France)
1972 .... IFBB Mr. Olympia (Germany)
1973 .... IFBB Mr. Olympia (U.S.A.)
1974 .... IFBB Mr. Olympia (U.S.A.)
1975 .... IFBB Mr. Olympia (South Africa)
1980 .... IFBB Mr. Olympia (Australia)

Appendix Two
Movie Career

1970 *Hercules in New York*
RAF Industries
Arthur A. Seidelman, director
Arnold Strong (Arnold Schwarzenegger), Deborah
Loomis

1973 *The Long Goodbye*
United Artists
Robert Altman, director
Elliott Gould, Sterling Hayden, Nina Van Pallandt

1976 *Stay Hungry*
United Artists
Bob Rafelson, director
Jeff Bridges, Sally Field, Arnold Schwarzenegger

1977 *Pumping Iron*
Cinema 5
George Butler, Robert Fiore, directors
Arnold Schwarzenegger, Lou Ferrigno, Franco
Columbo, Mike Katz

1979 *The Villain*
Columbia Pictures
Hal Needham, director
Kirk Douglas, Ann-Margret, Arnold Schwarzenegger

Appendix Two. Movie Career

1980 *The Jayne Mansfield Story* (TV movie)
CBS
Dick Lowry, director
Loni Anderson, Arnold Schwarzenegger, Raymond
Buktenica

1982 *Conan the Barbarian*
Universal Pictures
John Milius, director
Arnold Schwarzenegger, Max Von Sydow, James Earl
Jones, Sandahl Bergman

1984 *Conan the Destroyer*
Universal Pictures
Richard Fleischer, director
Arnold Schwarzenegger, Grace Jones, Wilt Chamberlain

1984 *The Terminator*
Orion Pictures
James Cameron, director
Arnold Schwarzenegger, Paul Winfield, Michael Biehn,
Linda Hamilton

1985 *Red Sonja*
MGM/UA
Richard Fleischer, director
Brigitte Nielsen, Arnold Schwarzenegger, Sandahl
Bergman

1985 *Commando*
Twentieth Century Fox
Mark Lester, director
Arnold Schwarzenegger, Rae Dawn Chong, Dan
Hedaya, Alyssa Milano

Appendix Two. Movie Career

1986 *Raw Deal*
    De Laurentiis
    John Irvin, director
    Arnold Schwarzenegger, Kathryn Harrold, Darren
    McGavin, Sam Wanamaker

1987 *Predator*
    Twentieth Century Fox
    John McTiernan, director
    Arnold Schwarzenegger, Carl Weathers, Jesse Ventura

1987 *The Running Man*
    Tri-Star
    Paul Michael Glaser, director
    Arnold Schwarzenegger, Richard Dawson, Maria
    Conchita Alonso

1988 *Red Heat*
    Tri-Star
    Walter Hill, director
    Arnold Schwarznegger, Jim Belushi, Peter Boyle

1988 *Twins*
    Universal
    Ivan Reitman, director
    Arnold Schwarzenegger, Danny DeVito, Kelly Preston,
    Chloe Webb

1990 "The Switch," episode of TV show, "Tales from the
    Crypt"
    HBO
    Arnold Schwarzenegger, director
    Kelly Preston, William Henry

Appendix Two. Movie Career

1990 *Total Recall*
Tri-Star
Paul Verhoeven, director
Arnold Schwarzenegger, Rachel Ticotin, Sharon Stone,
Ronny Cox

1990 *Kindergarten Cop*
Universal
Ivan Reitman, director
Arnold Schwarzenegger, Penelope Ann Miller, Pamela
Reed, Linda Hunt

1991 *Terminator 2: Judgment Day*
Tri-Star
James Cameron, director
Arnold Schwarzenegger, Linda Hamilton, Edward
Furlong, Robert Patrick, Joe Morton

1992 *Christmas in Connecticut* (TV movie)
TNT
Arnold Schwarzenegger, director
Dyan Cannon, Kris Kristofferson, Tony Curtis

1993 *The Last Action Hero*
Columbia Pictures
John McTiernan, director
Arnold Schwarzenegger, Austin O'Brien, Anthony
Quinn, Mercedes Ruehl

Source Notes

One. Arnold Schwarzenegger, the Boy
1. Kaye, Elizabeth. "Is All That Muscle All That Healthy?" *Family Health,* December 1977.
2. Schwarzenegger, Arnold. *Arnold: The Education of a Bodybuilder.* New York: Simon & Schuster, 1977.

Two. Bodybuilder-Soldier
1. Schwarzenegger, Arnold. *Arnold: The Education of a Bodybuilder.*

Three. Mr. Universe and Beyond
1. Butler, George. *Arnold Schwarzenegger: A Portrait.* New York: Simon & Schuster, 1990.

Four. Off to America
1. Wayne, Rick. *Muscle Wars: The Behind-the-Scenes Story of Competitive Bodybuilding.* New York: St. Martin's Press, 1985.
2. Gaines, Charles, and George Butler. *Pumping Iron: The Art and Sport of Bodybuilding.* New York: Simon & Schuster, 1981.
3. Wayne, Rick. *Muscle Wars.*

Five. Pumping Up
1. Mathews, Jack. "The Man Inside the Muscles." *Los Angeles Times,* September 3, 1989.

Source Notes

2. Kroll, Jack. "Brains and Brawn." *Newsweek,* May 17, 1976.

3. Christy, Marian. "Winning According to Schwarzenegger." *Boston Globe,* May 9, 1982.

Seven. In the Movies

1. Schickel, Richard. "A Delicate Beefcake Ballet." *Time,* January 24, 1977.

2. Clarens, Carlos. "Barbarians Now." *Film Comment,* May-June 1982.

3. Goodman, Joan. "Playboy Interview: Arnold Schwarzenegger." *Playboy,* January 1988.

Nine. Destroyer to Terminator

1. McGraw, Carol. "Schwarzenegger Flexes Muscles as U.S. Citizen." *Los Angeles Times,* September 18, 1983.

2. Rafferty, Terrence. "Terminated." *The New Yorker,* June 18, 1990.

3. Carr, Jay. "Here's a Total Recall of Schwarzenegger's Career." *Boston Globe,* June 28, 1991.

Ten. Taking Command

1. Richman, Alan. "Commando in Love." *People,* October 14, 1985.

Eleven. Making Some Deals

1. Coiner, Jill Brooke. "The Girl Who Got It All." *McCall's,* June 1992.

2. Wilmington, Michael. Review of *Predator. Los Angeles Times,* June 12, 1987.

3. Arnold Schwarzenegger talking about audience reaction to *Predator,* as quoted by Michael Blowen in "The Gentle Giant." *Boston Globe,* June 11, 1987.

Source Notes

Twelve. Running Man to Red Heat

1. Burke, Tom. "Sexy, Fun-Loving Schwarzenegger." *Cosmopolitan,* July 1988.
2. Ebert, Roger. Review of *Red Heat. New York Post,* June 17, 1988.
3. Mathews, Jack. "The Man Inside the Muscles." *Los Angeles Times,* September 3, 1989.
4. Coiner, Jill Brooke. "The Girl Who Got It All." *McCall's,* June 1992.
5. Prince, Susan. "Maria Shriver, No Kennedy Clone." *McCall's,* October 1988.
6. Coiner. "The Girl Who Got It All."
7. Olson, Wendy. "Schwarzenegger Gives Them a Lift." *Los Angeles Times,* June 2, 1987.

Thirteen. Arnold and His Twin

1. Mathews, Jack. "The Man Inside the Muscles." *Los Angeles Times,* September 3, 1989.
2. Murphy, Ryan. "Arnold Schwarzenegger: No Sweat." *Saturday Evening Post,* March 1989.
3. Koltnow, Barry. "From Conan to Cop: Pumped Up over Comedy." *San Francisco Examiner,* January 4, 1991.
4. Davis, Sally Ogle. "Tough Man, Tender Heart." *Redbook,* September 1990.
5. Ciotti, Paul. "Real Hollywood Muscle." *Los Angeles Times,* August 4, 1991.
6. Corliss, Richard. "Box-Office Brawn." *Time,* December 24, 1990.
7. Leahy, Michael. "Arnie Flexes His Muscles . . . Behind the TV Camera."

Fourteen. Conan Versus the Couch Potatoes

1. Ciotti, Paul. *Los Angeles Times,* August 4, 1991.

Source Notes

2. Coiner, Jill Brooke. *McCall's,* June 1992.

3. Murphy, Ryan. *Saturday Evening Post,* March 1989.

4. Rossellini, Lynn. "Pumping the Public Persona." *U.S. News & World Report,* November 26, 1990.

5. Carlson, Peter. "Pumping Hype." *Washington Post,* June 23, 1991.

6. Schwarzenegger, Arnold. "Kindergarten Cop Lays Down Law on Exercise." *The New York Times,* January 6, 1991.

Fifteen. Martian Spy to Kindergarten Cop

1. Mathews, Jack. *Los Angeles Times,* September 3, 1989.

2. Murphy, Ryan. *Saturday Evening Post,* March 1989.

3. Koltnow, Barry. *San Francisco Examiner,* January 4, 1991.

4. King, Susan. "Ivan Reitman, *Kindergarten Cop*'s Top Sergeant." *Los Angeles Times,* December 21, 1990.

5. McGuigan, Cathleen. "The Terminator Meets the Kindergartners." *Newsweek,* December 24, 1990.

6. Travers, Peter. Review of *Kindergarten Cop. Rolling Stone,* January 24, 1991.

Sixteen. Hasta la Vista, Baby!

1. Broeske, Pat H. "Well, He Did Say, 'I'll Be Back.' " *Los Angeles Times,* May 19, 1991.

2. Thompson, Anne. "Whatever Arnold Wants . . ." *Entertainment Weekly,* July 24, 1992.

3. Kelleher, Kathleen. "Men of Steel: For Arnold Schwarzenegger, It's No Sweat Taking Over for Joe Gold." *Los Angeles Times,* May 3, 1992.

For Further Reading

This list of books by and about Arnold Schwarzenegger just scratches the surface of the information available. A vast array of newspaper and magazine articles have also been written about him and more are written all the time.

Butler, George. *Arnold Schwarzenegger: A Portrait*. New York: Simon & Schuster, 1990.

Gaines, Charles, and George Butler. *Pumping Iron: The Art and Sport of Bodybuilding*. Revised and expanded edition. New York: Simon & Schuster, 1981.

Leigh, Wendy. *Arnold, an Unauthorized Biography*. Chicago: Congdon and Weed, 1990.

Robards, Brooks. *Arnold Schwarzenegger*. New York: Smithmark, 1992.

Schwarzenegger, Arnold, with Bill Dobbins. *Arnold's Bodybuilding for Men*. New York: Simon & Schuster, 1981.

Schwarzenegger, Arnold, with Bill Dobbins. *Encyclopedia of Modern Bodybuilding*. New York: Simon & Schuster, 1985.

Schwarzenegger, Arnold, with Charles Gaines. *Arnold's Fitness for Kids, Ages Birth–5*. New York: Bantam Doubleday Dell, 1993.

Schwarzenegger, Arnold, with Charles Gaines. *Arnold's Fitness for Kids, Ages 6–10*. New York: Bantam Doubleday Dell, 1993.

Schwarzenegger, Arnold, with Charles Gaines. *Arnold's Fit-*

For Further Reading

ness for Kids, Ages 11–14. New York: Bantam Doubleday Dell, 1993.

Schwarzenegger, Arnold, with Douglas Kent Hall. *Arnold's Bodybuilding for Women*. New York: Simon & Schuster, 1979.

Schwarzenegger, Arnold, with Douglas Kent Hall. *Arnold: The Education of a Bodybuilder*. New York: Simon & Schuster, 1977.

Wayne, Rick. *Muscle Wars: The Behind-the-Scenes Story of Competitive Bodybuilding*. New York: St. Martin's Press, 1985.

Index

Index

Index